Lyndon Publishing

Love by the Bushel

by

Janice Olson

For more information about me or my books, please visit my Website at: www.JaniceOlson.com, or email me at Janice at Janice Olson dot com

Thank you for choosing "Love by the Bushel." I believe you will enjoy Garrett's and Sage's journey to love.

And I would be remiss if I didn't give a shout out to my Beta Readers: Jackie, Jewlene, and Dana, and my editor, Kathleen Robinson for all your help whipping my book in shape. You ladies *save my bacon* time after time—you're great!

Thank you

Janice

Now enjoy the read.

Books by Janice Olson

Romantic Suspense: The Texas Sorority Sisters Series

Book 1 - Serenity's Deception
Book 2 - Lethal Intent
Book 3 - Chameleon
Book 4 - Run ... You Can't Hide
Book 5 - The Collector – Release 2017

Romance with a twist of humor: Texas Serendipity Series

Mr. What's-His-Name
Wanted A Man for Christmas
Airtight Case for Love
Singletude – Release 2017

The McCaslands of Primrose, Texas
2016 & 2017 ~ 5-book romance series

Love by the Bushel – Garrett McCasland
Arrested by Love – Justin McCasland
Don't Fence Me In – Nicholas (Nick) McCasland
Loves Comes Knocking – Matthew (Matt) McCasland
Love Comes Back to Town – Isobel (Issy) McCasland

On Sale November 1, 2017
A Sweet Noel ~ a contemporary romance novella
collection by seven authors. Look for my contribution:
"Sweet Christmas Setup"

Love by the Bushel

Chapter 1

Garrett McCasland

"Watch out!"

The warning came too late.

Out of nowhere, a huge basket of loose leaf lettuce ran into me as a woman's scream pierced my eardrums. I stumbled backward but caught myself at the last second. In the process, I dropped my hat and the tomato I'd just purchased from one of the vendors at McKinney's *Chestnut Square Farmer's Market*.

A pair of brown boots and shapely blue-jeaned legs flew into the air, along with the basket she carried. A flutter of green and purple leaves settled to the ground. The woman beneath the blanket of lettuce didn't move.

Squatting next to her, I began shoving the lettuce aside to see if she was conscious.

She began muttering loudly as her arms thrashed about. A fist connected with my eye, blinding me momentarily and smarted as good as any of my brothers' punches.

The young woman fought her way out from beneath the lettuce pile into a sitting position.

"What stupid idiot doesn't look where they're going." Pulling a clump of lettuce from her hair, she slung it to the ground and then glared at me with the most beautiful, brilliant green eyes I'd ever seen.

Momentarily stunned by the striking redheaded woman, I didn't speak. Instead, I stared dumbfounded.

Coming out of my stupor, I leaned forward to help her stand.

She leaned forward to get up.

Our heads collided.

"For Pete's sake, are you trying to kill me."

She shoved me, knocking me back on my rear. I got up, dusted my jeans off, then offered my hand to help her stand. "I'm so sorry. I didn't see you. I never meant—"

"You never meant what? To knock me down?" She spat out a purple leaf while slapping my hand away. "I don't need your help. You've helped quite enough, thank you."

She continued to mutter about incompetent, stupid, inept, clumsy men, while she shoved to her feet.

At her full height, the top of her head came to my chin. She was shapely in all the right places, and a good five years younger than me, closer to my sister, Issy's age.

I shook my head. Why was I even cataloging this spitfire? I'd have to be completely out of my mind to look twice at a woman with a temper as bad as hers.

Come on, be civil.

"Are you all right?"

"What do you think, after charging into me and knocking me down?"

"Lady, there's no need to be rude. I wasn't—"

"*Rude? Rude?*" She scowled. "You've got to be kidding me. You call me rude when you run me down, and then just about knock me senseless."

She glanced down and then waved her hand at the mess surrounding her feet. "And just look what you've done. This was half of my lettuce sales for the day and now it's trash."

"I'm sorry, but—"

11

"Sorry? Sorry doesn't fix it. What do you expect me to do? Sell mangled lettuce?"

"Listen, Lady, I'm trying to apologize, but you won't let me. I didn't bump into you intentionally."

She gave an insolent snort. "No, you just can't be bothered to watch where you're walking. With that attitude, you would probably trip over one of the little ones walking around here."

I looked around. There were quite a few spectators chuckling. One man had the nerve to laugh out loud. I felt like punching the guy since I couldn't punch the object of my anger.

She had gone too far.

"I have no intention of tripping over a child. And the accident was as much your fault as it was mine." I pulled out my wallet and dug through my money before holding out two twenties and a ten. "Here, this should pay for your loss."

She looked at the money greedily, then gave an emphatic shake of her head. "Not likely."

"What? This is not enough? Exactly what is your lettuce made of, gold?"

I couldn't believe she could be so mercenary. I dug into my wallet again and held out double the amount. "Well, this is as much as I'm willing to pay. Any more than that, lady, and you can sue me."

The redhead looked ready to tear into me.

"I wouldn't take your money if I was starving and didn't have a dime to my name. Have a better day than you've made mine." She turned, then bent to grab the basket a few feet away. "And I'll feel fortunate if I never lay eyes on you again."

I would have loved to let her have it for her rude behavior, but I clamped my mouth shut.

"Take the money. You know what he's offering is more than fair. And it *was* an accident." One booth over, the older woman wore a worried look.

"Stay out of this, Maude." The young woman stomped around the table where other vegetables were already sitting in neat, appealing rows, along with golden jars of honey. She dropped the basket, kicking it under the table, before stomping off toward the parking lot.

I turned to Maude. "Hi, I'm Garrett McCasland."

"Nice to meet yah. I'm Maude Jenkins."

"Is this her table?" I nodded in the direction the young woman had gone.

"It sure is." Maude had a glint in her eyes.

I handed her the wad of bills I'd offered earlier. "When she comes back, would you please give this to her? It's more than fair compensation."

"Sure will. And I agree, it's more than fair. Thanks." Maude pursed her lips. "She won't admit it, but she needs this money."

Looking around for my Stetson, I found it in the dirt. The tomato I purchased was splattered next to it, the juicy innards covered a portion of the brim. Scowling at the disgusting mess, I picked up my Stetson and flicked off as much of the tomato as I could.

"By the looks of it, that redheaded spitfire has also cost me a Stetson."

"At times, she is that." Maude cackled. "Here." She pulled a wad of wipes from a small round tub, holding them out to me. "Use half of those to gently wipe the gunk off, and the other to finish the cleaning."

"Thanks. But I think it's past redemption."

Maude rolled her eyes, snorting. "If you'll do what I say, you'll see your hat'll be as good as new."

"I'll give it a try. Thanks." Seeing the feisty redhead coming back up the slight incline again, carrying another basket of lettuce, I sidestepped the mess made earlier. Then I hurried off in the opposite direction without a backward glance.

Since I'd given more than enough money to cover her sales and a hefty amount besides, I felt I had dealt fairly with the woman. And if she didn't think so, that wasn't my problem.

The woman would have been pretty if it hadn't been for her rotten attitude and her stinkin' disposition. She'd also do well to fix that wild mop of red hair.

No matter. If I ever lay eyes on her again, it would be *too* soon.

Chapter 2

Sage Anderson

Where did that guy get off calling me rude? He was the one who needed some manners.

I took a deep breath. It didn't do much to calm my temper as I watched the man walk away without so much as a backward glance, or a *may I help you clean this up?*

I stomped my foot. "Who does that guy think he is? Mr. Money Bags, handing out cash like it's paper?"

"Sage Anderson, you've let your temper get the best of you. He was only trying to make up for what you lost, which, in my opinion, was decent of the man. He really didn't owe you squat since both of you were to fault."

"That may be true. But ..." I averted my face not wanting Maude to see how the truth of her words stung. Grabbing the empty basket, I got to the task of cleaning up the lettuce.

Maude cackled. "He sure wasn't bad on the eyes. If I'd been a few years younger, I would have been inclined to bat my lashes at him. Or better yet, ask him to my place for dinner."

The outrageous picture of Maude flirting with Mr. Money Bags had me chuckling, but it didn't ease my guilt.

"You have my permission to bat your lashes all you want. I'll look for someone who doesn't think he can walk on water."

"*Hmm,* that man sure got to you. You know, you could do a whole lot worse."

A snort was my response to her outrageous suggestion.

I scooped up an arm full of lettuce and shoved it into the bushel basket, then marched over to dump the mess into the trash. After several more trips to the trashcan, and then one more to my truck, I was ready for business.

My insides were still smarting—more from the embarrassment of my behavior than from my loss.

Pulling out my canvas chair, I positioned it so I could watch for customers, yet stay in the shade. My mind nagged at how stupidly I'd handled the incident earlier. When would I learn to think before speaking? I could have used the money he offered. Just another example of one of the dumbest things I've done.

I sucked in a breath, wrapping my arms around my stomach. The old familiar burning started out slow in my gut, then hit with a vengeance. If it were only me. But I had Grams to think about. And I needed every last cent to stay afloat. But no! My stubborn pride stepped in, which was more than foolhardy.

When would I learn to use the sense God gave me?

I waited on customers, made change, and bagged produce until closing. All during that time, I looked for the man, wanting to apologize, but never saw him. More than likely, he purposely steered clear of my area for fear I'd tear into him again.

My face heated when I thought of the guy telling his wife, if he had one, about his encounter with the madwoman at *Chestnut Square*. For some reason the thought of him being married and laughing about what took place ate at me.

As Maude had observed, the guy really wasn't bad looking. In fact, he had a handsome smile to match the sparkle in his brilliant blue eyes, even if his hair did need a trim. And after I'd tried his patience, he still attempted to make it right.

Shame on me.

Grams always said my Anderson pride and fiery temper would be my ruination. Today was a perfect example of both at work causing me loss. As it was, I couldn't feel worse.

I loaded the last of what little produce I had in the back of my old pickup. I pulled my tarp over everything and then tied it down before walking back up the hill to see if Maude needed a hand.

"I was awaitin' on you. I didn't want to give this to you until I knew you had simmered down some." Maude held out a wad of money.

"Where did that come from?" The sinking suspicion I already knew, left a bitter taste in my mouth, much like an unripe persimmon.

"The young fellow handed it to me. Said to give it to you for the lettuce he'd ruined."

"Oh, Maude." Shaking my head, tears pricked my eyelids. Earlier, I didn't think I could feel worse, but the money Maude held out proved me wrong.

"Don't you shake your head at me, young lady."

Maude took hold of my hand, prying open my fingers, and then slapped the wad in my palm.

"And don't you dare try to give it back. It's yours. Not mine."

"But I was awful to the man."

"You were. But that don't change the fact, the money is still yours." She nodded emphatically. "Now put it away."

"Thanks, Maude."

"Don't thank me. It's the man you should be thankin'"

"I would if I could." I lowered my head, so ashamed.

"Well, next time, if there is a next time … you'll know what to do."

"Yeah, I do. And I will. I'm not perfect, but I'm working on it." My heart sunk as I gave Maude a hug. "I'll see you next market."

"Sure thing."

Once I got inside my truck, I couldn't stop my hand from digging the wad out of my pocket. My heart raced, as my shaky fingers unrolled the bills. A faint smell of sandalwood cologne rose from the money, bringing up an image of the man.

I began counting—twenty, forty, sixty, eighty, one hundred.

This can't be right.

I looked around as if the man was standing there watching me. He wasn't, of course.

Counting the money again, I found two of the bills had stuck together, twice, making the total one hundred forty dollars. My heart sank. Both bushel baskets combined, if I could have completely sold out, would have only been worth, at the most, ninety dollars for the lot. But one-hundred-forty was over the top and excessively generous.

He couldn't have known what he gave Maude. Or did he?

I gave another quick look around. No avenging gargoyle, no good looking stranger, no one standing there asking for the money. The gravity of the situation caused tears to stream down my face.

One hundred and forty dollars might not mean much to some folks, including the cowboy, but to me, it meant the difference between being able to make the mortgage payment and not.

At this juncture in life, every penny counted, every bit of produce mattered. And what I didn't sell, if I could freeze, pickle, or can, I did. Just another way of keeping food on the table, or giving me something extra to sell. And the produce that wouldn't keep, I gave it to the woman's shelter in town.

Every day, I worked hard to keep Grams and me on her farm, regardless if it was mortgaged to the hilt. And so far, I had been truly blessed.

"Thanks, Cowboy, whoever you are. Come back and dump my lettuce anytime you want. And I promise I won't tear your head off next time."

I laughed while wiping my face. I drove to the office to pay the rent for the next market.

Inside, Sally was bent over, looking in a box.

"Hey, Sally." I pulled out the rent money, handing it to her.

"Did you do well today?" Her look of concern was touching.

"Yes." *Thanks to a stranger.* "It started out a bit rough. But by the end, I did very well."

Sally slid the receipt across the desk along with a flyer. "You might be interested in this. If not, recycle it. Have a good one and a safe trip home."

"Will do. Have a great weekend." I folded the advertisement, sticking it in my pocket.

Within thirty minutes, I was home and backed up to the barn. Old Sammy, our border collie, followed the truck the whole way, barking and jumping.

After stepping out of the truck, I gave Sammy a good ol' rub.

"How are you, boy? Did you keep Grams safe while I was gone?"

He barked, then followed me back and forth to the barn where I unloaded my leftover vegetables into the two old refrigerators. Getting tired of the game, Sammy ran off to the back porch to lie down while I fed the chickens, and did some more chores. It was close to four-thirty by the time I got into the truck and headed back up to the house.

Grams met me on the porch to give me a hug. "I'll have dinner ready at five."

"Thanks, but I'm not all that hungry."

"You have to eat, Sage, otherwise, you'll get sick. You're already too skinny as it is."

"Thanks for worrying about me." I walked into the mudroom, kicked off my boots, then in my stocking feet I entered the kitchen.

"Let me dump my stuff in my room and wash up. We'll talk over dinner."

"All right. Maybe you can get to bed early and get some much needed rest."

"If only. I've got the accounting to do."

I made my way up the stairs, the thoughts of what took place earlier with the good-looking cowboy still weighed heavy on my mind. Inside my bedroom I dropped my cash box on the desk, shaking my head. I figured I'd never get the opportunity to set the wrong to right. I'd never see him again.

When I entered the bath room to wash up, I gave a longing look at the claw-foot tub. A good soak would do my aching body wonders.

"Tonight, you and I have a date."

I caught a glimpse of myself in the mirror and shuddered. Surely I didn't look this bad this morning.

After washing up, I ran a brush through my hair before pulling it back into a bushy ponytail.

I snatched up the advertisement from the Chestnut Square office, unfolding it while going downstairs. The word Aquaponics snagged my attention. It was something I was interested in but knew it would take money to implement—money we didn't have.

An Introduction to Aquaponic Gardening
Tired of tilling your land?
Looking for a new approach to organic vegetables?
Try Aquaponics
Whether farming small or by the acre
Aquaponics is the answer to growing organic vegetables
For information or to Register for next Saturday's class:
Call: Garrett at: 872-555-4489

Grams was sitting at the table when I came into the kitchen. The plates were dished up, and the glasses filled with sweet iced tea. The aromas triggered my waning appetite.

When Grams blessed the food, she prayed for my tired body and spirit.

I didn't understand how she did it, but she always knew when I was discouraged or upset about something.

"What you got there, hon?" Grams stared at the ad I'd set on the table.

I picked it up, staring at it before placing it on the table again. "It's an advertisement for a class on Aquaponics."

"Aqua-what?" Gram's sweet face was all scrunched up.

"It's a relatively new way of raising organic crops in water. I've read some about it, but would like to learn more. I'm sure the class will be too expensive though." I shoved the ad toward Grams while taking a bit of creamy mashed potatoes and gravy.

She read it, then scooted it back to me.

"You might be surprised. Call." Grams hiked that one brow of hers—emphasizing her point.

"I'll think about."

Grams nibbled on her food asking me about my day.

I explained about the man, the lettuce, *and* the money.

"I would say the Good Lord was watching out for you today."

"I didn't think so at the time, but when I got into the truck and counted the hundred and forty dollars, I cried. I knew He had, even if I wasn't exactly nice to the man." I leaned back in the chair, grimacing. "I confess. I was downright rude."

Grams pursed her lips. "You did apologize, right?"

Her words made me feel like a child again, wanting to run and hide my face instead of confessing the truth.

"I never got the chance. He walked away thinking I was the worst possible human being on planet earth. And then later when Maude gave me the wad of money,"—I bit my lower lip while my stomach knotted—"I felt like a heel. Grams, I treated him horribly."

She patted my hand. "Well, sweetie, you're overworked and overtired, is what. But since you can't apologize to the man, you're just gonna have to forgive yourself and go on from here. Chalk it up to a lesson well learned." Grams breathed in. "You can't allow your temper to match your hair." She stood, rested her hand on my shoulder, and then took her plate to the sink.

My appetite ruined, I followed her. Grams placed her things in the dishwasher—the one thing I insisted on buying, against her protests, when I moved in and took over the farm.

She brushed a few stray white hairs back from her wrinkled face. "Well, I'm a bit tired. I think I'll read a little, and then go to bed. Don't you stay up too late, ya' hear?"

"I won't." I picked up the aquaponic advertisements, reading it over again.

"You'd be smart to give that Garrett person a call if you're really interested." Grams stood in the doorway. "You won't know the cost until you ask."

I shrugged.

"Who knows, that Aqua-thing might be a whole lot easier than what you have to do now. Or you could reconsider your mom's offer. You'd have it a whole lot easier."

Giving a snort of disgust, I said, "Not hardly. I won't take a job in Dallas and let her ship you off to an old folks' home. I'll stay right where I am. And so will you."

She pointed at the brochure on the table. "Well, at least call and see what the class costs."

"I just might. 'Night, Grams."

"No might. You do as I say."

"Yes, ma'am." I smiled at Grams retreating back.

Her steps were a little slower, her shoulders a little more slumped, which caused worry to gnaw at my gut. Next week, I would call the doctor and have Grams go in for a checkup.

I read the ad again, all the while wondering if I should call. Our situation being what it was, I couldn't afford anything extra, let alone buy the material it would take to start a system the size I would need. I tapped the ad with my nail.

What could it hurt?

Punching in the number, I pulled my bottom lip through my teeth waiting for the call to go through.

"Garrett McCasland, speaking."

"Hi. I picked up one of your advertisement from the Chestnut Square market and was wondering about the classes and the cost."

"The class is this coming Saturday at nine a.m. No cost. It's an introduction to aquaponics. I'll show you my setup, explain how it works, and tell you the pros and cons of the system. I've found very few cons and a lot of pros." He chuckled.

I liked the sound of his voice and his easy manner. "Did you say no charge?"

"Yes. I want to generate interest. My classes are hands-on, meaning everyone participates. Would you like me to put you down?"

"Well, ah-sure." I wound a strand of hair around my finger.

"Make sure you dress comfortable, wear work shoes or boots, sunscreen, and maybe a hat to keep the sun from blistering your head."

The line when silent.

"How many do you have enrolled?"

"One."

"Me? Am I the only one?" I wasn't sure about taking a class by myself.

"Well, at the moment, yes. However, I just put out the flyers today. I expect more will be calling to join the class."

By the time I hung up, I was more than ready for a hot soak in the tub.

I undressed for my bath and noticed a black and blue mark on my hip. My mind automatically returned to the man who had pricked my conscience off and on all day.

I stepped into the tub, sinking down to my neck, allowing the warmth to seep deep into my sore muscles. Resting my head against the back of the tub, I closed my eyes.

The image of a man's sexy smile, sparkling blue eyes, and wavy brown hair kissed by the sun, made me long for something I figured I'd never find. Pure, unadulterated love. The kind to last a lifetime. The kind that accepts you for who you are without wanting to change you.

Was Cowboy that kind of guy? I wasn't likely to find out. If he ever laid eyes on me again he'd probably hightail it in the opposite direction.

Chapter 3

Garrett

When would Isobel learn that I won't date one of her girlfriends, regardless how many she brings around? This one makes what? Four, five?

I've quit counting.

And what was this one's name? Oh, yeah, Cassandra. Cassie for short.

The girl, though made up like one of those Hollywood stars, didn't look old enough to be out of high school, let alone chasing after a grown man.

"Would you mind passing the rolls?"

Why did her question sound more like entrapment? My inclination was to throw her a roll, but I knew Mom would come down on me like a ton of bricks. I ignored her, that is, until my brother Nick jabbed me in the ribs, chuckling.

"Roll? Sure." I handed her the basket without eye contact, then went back to eating.

"Isobel said you're an aquaphonics gardener." Cassie's silly laugh unnerved me

The way she batted her eyes, there was a good chance one of her fake lashes might give way and land in her food. *Come to think of it that might provide some good entertainment.*

I released my breath. "Aquaponics. There's no 'h'. It's aq-ua-pon-ics."

"Oh, sorry. It's so similar."

"Yet, so far away." I didn't bother keeping the scorn from my voice.

The girl's tinkling laughter was driving me crazy. I glanced across the table at Issy, giving her a look of … *are you kidding?*

"What exactly do you do with the aqua-ah—" She wrinkled her brow.

"Aq-ua-pon-ics. I'm a plain ol' farmer." *Maybe that would chase her off.*

"He's more than a farmer." Issy narrowed her eyes in my direction. "He has one of the most innovative setups in the country. People come from all over to see his operation. He also teaches at the community college and lectures around the U.S."

Issy all but stuck her tongue out at me.

I was impressed that Issy knew so much about my farm. She even sounded proud, which made me feel a little kinder toward her.

"Aquaponics is farming. It's a system of raising produce without tilling the land. So you see, it's all the same. I'm a glorified farmer."

"You're more like certifiable."

My brother Matthew's verbal jab missed the intended mark. By now, I was used to him finding fault with how I earned my living. He was still upset that I went into farming instead of staying on as a partner in his law firm.

After being an attorney for two years, I found out being cooped up in an office all day wasn't my idea of a life.

"Certifiable, maybe, but I enjoy the work I do." I gave Matt a huge smile. "I'm single, and answer to no one but myself, and that's how I like it." The last I directed to little Cassie.

"Oh. How fascinating." Again, her over-the-top flirting was ridiculous.

"Well, now, some would say what Matt here does is far more fascinating and far more lucrative."

Matt gave me a beady-eyed warning.

"In fact, being the oldest in the family, I would think he's just about ready to find a wife and settle down."

I smiled sweetly at Matt. I knew good manners dictated that he'd stay seated, when what he'd rather do was come around the table, yank me out of my chair to drag me outside for a free-for-all.

"No. That's where you're wrong." Matt bared his teeth. "I'm a confirmed bachelor."

"Cassie, what is your profession?" Mom's diplomatic intervention wasn't lost on any of us except Cassie.

"Well, Daddy doesn't think I need to be in a hurry to find a profession. He says to just take my time, and something will come to me. So I guess you could say, I'm in between jobs, except I never had my first one." She laughed.

The dropping of Mom's jaw had us all silently chuckling.

"Cassie's father is in oil. And Cassie is an only child." Issy took a frustrated breath, knowing she'd lost yet another chance to get one of her brothers married off.

"Oh, I see." Mom clearly didn't see, but let the subject drop.

"It's a shame Justin, our third brother, couldn't make it to family dinner. I think you and he would have really hit it off." I tried to keep from smiling.

"Justin?" Cassie looked a bit confused.

"He's the policeman I told you about." Issy gave me a *you better watch your back* look.

I raised my brows. *Touché.*

"Oh, yeah, I remember. Well, if I ever get stopped for speeding, I'll be sure to mention I'm a friend of the family." Cassie smiled, tossing her dark hair over her shoulder.

The girl wasn't half bad on the eyes, just needed a few more years to grow up, if she ever would.

"Justin is dating a girl in town. Or at least he was the last time I saw him, unlike my other three brothers," Issy threw back.

"Don't include me in on this." Nick leaned back in his chair, looking a little worried. "I'm like Matt, I'm a confirmed bachelor. Just me and my longhorns. I don't have the time or energy for a woman."

"Well, Mom, I hate to eat and run, but I need to get back and prepare for tomorrow's class." I stood.

"You can't wait for dessert?"

"Afraid not." I patted my trim stomach. "I'm already full."

"I didn't know you were teaching on Saturdays now." Issy looked a little suspicious.

"Afraid so. It's a meetup."

She probably thought I was ducking out on her sweet little setup — *come meet my brother, Garrett. He's looking for a wife.* Which I wasn't

Issy hadn't fooled anyone, especially me. This was her get even with Garrett time, since I spoiled her date with that guy from Dallas last week. He had all the wrong reasons for sniffing around my baby sister.

"I hope you're not stretching yourself too thin." Mom's brows crunched together.

"Kayla, he's a grown man. Leave him be." Dad shook his head.

"I know he's grown, Gavin, but ...." Her voice got a little testy.

"I'm only doing an introductory class, trying to get other commercial and small truck farms interested in changing, or at least thinking about aquaponics. So far, I have eight enrolled, which isn't too bad for the first class."

I gave her a reassuring smile. "This class will be fun. For once, I'll have help to build another portion of my beds, enlarging my growing area. And the good part, it's all free labor."

Feeling a little sorry for Cassie's unsuspecting part in my sister's thwarted scheme, I smiled at her. "It was nice to meet you, Cassie. Keep looking. I'm sure you'll find a goal for your life." *And a man.*

Stopping by Mom's chair, I gave her a hug and a kiss on the cheek. "Thanks, Mom. As usual, the meal was superb. 'Night all."

I grabbed my Stetson off the hat rack in the hall and made my escape out the front door.

Issy might play her little games with me, but that wouldn't stop me from chasing off any male predator that might come around my little sister. Only the best man would do for her. But I didn't know where that man might be found. *What a shame.*

The sky was pitch black, the lights from my Chevy truck reached no better than a hundred yards in front of me. Though I only lived a couple of miles from the homestead, I kept my eyes peeled for deer and stray cattle crossing the road.

Not often, but sometimes, like tonight, my house seemed a hundred miles from all living beings. The farther I got from the McCasland homestead, the lonelier it became. Maybe it was time I thought about settling down and looking for a wife. But where would I look?

Certainly not any of the girls Issy brought around. None of them stirred me enough to pursue them. I shook my head to dislodge the image of the redheaded spitfire from last Saturday. She'd sure make life interesting.

We all knew what Issy was up to by trying to marry us off. She believed she'd have a free pass to date whomever she pleased.

Well, little princess, you've got another think coming.

Regardless if we all got married tomorrow, we'd still scrutinize the guys, and probably run off the lot of them. We'd be hard put to find someone good enough for our little Princess Isobel.

I made the turn into the long drive back to my place.

When I built my house, I had a large family in mind, much like my parents had with us five kids.

Building the house was the easy part. Finding a woman, now that was a challenge. If I didn't find her soon, I just might have to take a closer look at Issy's friends.

No, on second thought, I'll pass. I want a woman I can enjoy, respect, and love enough to be married to her for a lifetime.

If the redhead from the market hadn't been such a loose cannon, I might have looked at her more than once.

Chapter 4

Sage

"What's that saying, Grams? *Early to bed, early to rise, makes a man healthy, wealthy, and wise.* At least I possess one of the three. Healthy." I laughed. "At the rate I'm going, the other two won't ever come."

I took a sip of coffee that I allowed to turn lukewarm while mulling over our financial problems.

"Now, Sage, don't you go getting discouraged. You have to count your blessings. We're a lot better off than some." Grams sat at the breakfast table, looking off at nothing in particular.

She smiled, turning her gaze on me. "There's never a day that I don't thank God for bringing you here to live with me. You're doing such a fine job keeping us in food and a roof over our heads, even if it's tough going at times.

"Thanks, Grams." I frowned. "But here lately it seems harder to make ends meet, no matter how hard I try."

"Well, now, maybe this meeting thing you're going to will help you find an easier path."

"It's only a pipedream, Grams. I'll never have enough money laid aside to buy the things I'll need to put the plan into action. But thankfully, we still have our land and a roof over our heads. And I can dream."

I gave Grams a hug. "I've got to get on the road or I'll be late. Thanks for packing my lunch. I'll see you later this afternoon."

Betsy, the beat up old 66' Chevy truck, was brand new when Gramps bought her. When he passed away, the truck sat in the barn, covered with a tarp, until I moved back on the farm with Grams.

Being our only mode of transportation, I bartered with one of the mechanics in Primrose — vegetables and canned goods, and a half side of beef, in exchange for work on Betsy and teaching me how to do minor repairs.

My bartering paid off by me being able to keep my truck in good running condition with little or no cost to me.

I released a breath, knowing by next year's inspection the truck would need tires, otherwise, I'd be walking the seven miles into town. It didn't seem like I would ever catch a break.

Slowing down, I read the address on the ornate mailbox, and then looked at my scribbled note I'd copied from the email. I grimaced. Yup. This was the place.

I turned into the drive and drove through the arched gateway over a metal cattle guard. I had watched this house being built with admiration and a small spark of envy. I now knew who owned it, or at least I would soon meet the man.

Whoever this Garrett fellow was, he had some bucks. Unlike our place, he had no rundown house or barn in need of paint and repairs. By the looks of his spread, he was what they would call a gentleman farmer.

The house, a huge two-story McMansion, was built in an old Victorian farmhouse style with a large wraparound porch. Not that I was envious, *well, maybe a little*. But I wouldn't envy his wife cleaning the monstrosity. It would take a month of Sundays to clean the place from top to bottom.

I pulled around behind the white barn as instructed in the email I had received, and saw several large, semitransparent round-top greenhouses with the sides rolled up. Beneath the tent-like structures were rows and rows of vibrant plants.

Seeing several late model trucks and cars lined up, I pulled up alongside a brand new Ford truck. None of the vehicles were of ol' Betsy's vintage. *Come to think of it, just about anything would be new compared to Betsy.*

I patted Betsy's dash. "Don't you dare let these big boys intimidate you or make you feel inferior. You're still precious in my sight. I love you, gal."

I wasn't sure if I was saying it for Betsy's benefit or to bolster my own self-worth.

Turning off the engine, I grimaced once again while I waited for Betsy to stop dieseling and announce our arrival.

Sure enough, as if on cue, Betsy backfired, letting lose a blast that sounded more like a shotgun fired up close and personal. Some distance away, several people in the little crowd jumped, while *everyone* looked in our direction.

My face filled with heat, as I climbed down out of the truck, then shut the door.

"Well, if they didn't know we were here before, they do now."

Ramming my old floppy hat down on my head, I headed in the direction of the covered greenhouses. I glanced around, taking in McCasland's sweet setup. No halfway measures here. Not even a respectable weed would be caught growing among his green pastures.

Second thoughts about attending this meetup flew through my head as I sauntered over to where several men and one woman were standing talking. My insides quivered, feeling out of my element, while I wondered which one was Garrett and if I was the only newbie here?

One thing for sure, I figured I was the only one who couldn't afford to set up a little aqua system, let alone, one a tenth the size this McCasland guy had.

Everyone turned when I approached. I smiled. "Hi, I'm Sage. Am I late?"

One rather good-looking young man pulled away from the men and moved closer to me, grinning from ear-to-ear.

"No. I'd say you're just in time." He stuck out his hand. "Hi, I'm JD Random. This here is, Frank, my brother." He thumbed back over his shoulder.

The younger Random nodded his greeting, barely looking at me. JD made up for his younger brother's bashfulness by holding my hand a little too long.

"Hi, Sage, I'm Sibyl Johnson, and this is Ken, my husband." The woman stuck out her hand, giving me a friendly smile. Her dark-brown hair was cut pixie style, and she was probably ten years my senior, but I liked her right off.

"Nice to meet you."

Sibyl's warm welcome helped to dissolve my awkward feelings.

The crunch of gravel had everyone turning to see who had walked up.

"Well, if I've properly counted heads, I think we're all here. I'm Garrett McCasland, and welcome to my aquaponics farm."

I stood at the back of the small group and couldn't see Garrett over their heads. However, his voice was familiar, *too* familiar. Then it hit me. I knew where I'd heard his voice before. My heart dropped into the pit of my stomach, and I wanted to turn and run.

Garrett McCasland was the lettuce *guy*. The one who collided with me at the Chestnut Market last Saturday. The one who had given me all that money. The one I had said despicable things to, and had yet to apologize for my actions.

At least now, I could put a face to the name on the brochure — Garrett McCasland.

I knew one thing for sure, fate was definitely against me by playing this ugly trick.

Fortunately, I was at the back and Garrett hadn't seen me … *yet*. I hunched down lower, doing my best to prolong the moment when he realized I was on his property and in his meetup.

Would he throw me off his land? I prayed not.

"Over the next five hours, I want to impart my love for aquaponics to you. However, first, I'd like to begin with introductions. Please give me your name, where you're from, why you're here, and why you're interested in aquaponics."

I figured I was safe for about as long as it took all the others to get through their introductions for Garrett to realize I was in his midst. Four or five minutes, ten tops, if I was lucky.

Should I just sneak off and run before he realized I was here?

No, I won't run.

Like a glutton for humiliation, I stayed put, hunched down out of Garrett's sight.

One by one the introductions were made. What they said didn't register with me. I was too worried Garrett would degrade me in front of everyone like I did him at the market.

As the time drew nearer for me to be introduced, I gave more thought to taking the chicken's way out.

Made of sterner stuff, or just plain stupid, I wasn't sure, I stayed put. After all, I was an

Anderson. Strong, invincible, and … at the present moment shaking in my boots.

Finally, the last person, JD finished with his intro. And like I had often imagined the Biblical account of the Red Sea parting for the children of Israel, everyone split apart and left me standing alone and naked.

Well, I really wasn't naked, more like exposed.

I was unprotected from the shocked, judging eyes of Garrett McCasland.

Giving a weak smile, I said, "Hi. I'm Sage Anderson." I bolstered my smile into a full-fledged grin. "I believe we have already met, although not formally introduced."

He did well concealing that split-second of shock that didn't go unnoticed by me.

"Ah, yes, we have met before. So *you're* Sage Anderson." His face showed no signs of anger, yet there was a harshness in his eyes.

The incredulous sound of his voice would have been laughable if my insides weren't quaking and on the verge of puking up my breakfast.

I bit my lip before answering. "Afraid so."

"Well, *Sage*, tell us about yourself, why you're here. And I suppose, you have a good reason."

Garrett's last remark and Sybil's muted gasp put a backbone in me where there was little before.

"Certainly, I have a *good* reason. I'm a truck farmer looking for a better way to grow my food and come out with a superior product."

"And you're from where?"

His narrow-eyed stare had my backbone collapsing.

You will not cower before this man, even if you do owe him an apology.

I stiffened my spine. "I live less than five minutes down that road." I pointed out to the road in front of Garrett's property. "You could say we're practically neighbors."

"Hopefully, not that close."

The collective sound of shock had Garrett turning a little pink—if I'm allowed to use that word to describe his less than manly color. However, he recovered faster than a roadrunner sprinting across a busy highway.

"Well, since we seem to all be acquainted, shall we go on a tour of the farm?"

Without another look in my direction, he started walking toward one of the six greenhouses. A couple of the men fell into step with him and began talking.

If I were going to escape, now would be the time. I was on the verge of turning around when Sybil took hold of my arm.

"I guess we better follow the men." Sybil smiled too brightly, like she knew a secret, or wanted to know mine.

"Sure. Why not." There was nothing to do but to fall into step with her—that or have her drag me all the way to the greenhouse, which I wouldn't allow.

"I'm so glad you came. I told Ken I would feel out of place if I were the only woman in the group. But you saved me from feeling awkward. Thanks, Sage."

"Don't mention it."

"Before the day's over, you'll have to tell me what that back there was all about." She nodded in the direction we had left. "I just know there's a juicy story there waiting to be told." Her eyes twinkled, and her grin was positively huge.

"Let's just say, our first meeting was less than auspicious. I didn't know who Garrett was, or I wouldn't have come today.

Sybil looked at me strangely, a question on the tip of her tongue.

"Oh, nothing bad about him. I just owe the man an apology for being so rude the first time we met."

"Like I said, maybe over lunch, you and I can go off from the others and you can tell me all the juicy details." She gave me a conspirator's wink.

I chuckled. "There's nothing juicy about it. Let's just leave it at, I'm the last person on earth Garrett wanted to see in his class today. And if I had any decency left in me, I'd get in my truck and go home."

Her hold on my arm became stronger.

"Oh, no you don't. You're here, and now you've gotta stay. Come on." She pulled me in the direction where the men had already disappeared. "You're made of strong stock, the kind that won't let anyone chase you off before you get what you're after." Sybil winked at me.

I wasn't sure what she referred to … *the meetup or Garrett.*

Chapter 5

Garrett

Like something out of a nightmare, there stood Sage, the woman I wouldn't forget, and wished to never see again. I'll admit, I'd thought of her many times during the week. Yet not in a favorable light.

Why hadn't I asked who she was when she enrolled? It would have saved me a day full of irritation.

Her actions of a week ago were still fresh in my mind. For some reason she carried a certain fascination I couldn't shake. More like the beauty of a rattlesnake — tail rattling, tongue slipping in and out, that deadly stare before it strikes.

Yep! That was Sage. A beauty she might be, but for certain, more dangerous than anything I'd ever encountered.

Surprisingly, throughout my lecture and even during the question and answer period, she was quiet and kept her distance. She stayed at the back of the pack using them as a protective barrier between her and me as if she were cautious, uncertain what I might say or do.

I should be the one wary of her, the way she flew off the handle. The woman couldn't be sane, regardless of how enticing she might be.

All through the day, I did my best to not let Sage distract me, but it was hard not to look her way and see her thoughts. Her enthusiasm for the process made me feel a little kinder toward her, but still …

"Since I know some of you sell at the Chestnut Market in McKinney and other places, I've set up my classes for the off weeks of the market. So, if you want more hands-on learning, sign up for the next class. And if you know anyone else who might be interested, please let them know about the classes. We'll meet two more times."

"My size of operation may not be what you're looking for, but you can scale the size either up or down to fit your needs. I'll see you in two weeks. But if you have any questions, I'll stick around for a little while longer to answer them. Enjoy the rest of your day."

Seeing Sage was about to leave, I said, "Sage, I'd like a moment of your time when I'm through."

She turned, looking at me, her eyes huge, wild, as if she was ready to bolt to her car. "I really need to get—"

"I'll only take a few minutes of your time, please." Why I was being a glutton for more punishment, I couldn't fathom.

"All right." None too happy, she turned to Sybil and they began talking.

I kept an eye on her while I answered some of the guys' questions to make sure she didn't leave. When I saw she was getting impatient, I said, "Listen, I don't want to hold Sage any longer, so if you have more questions, email them to me."

Sage hugged Sybil and I heard her say, "See you next time."

So she was coming back. I wasn't sure if I was glad or wished she'd hated the class and wouldn't return. One thing for certain, I wanted to know what her intentions were for showing up here in the first place. Did she know this was my farm, my meetup?

JD walked over to Sage and began talking and laughing. For some reason his easiness with her didn't set well with me. He was a bit too friendly. And Sage was a little too quick to smile at the man.

What did they think I was running here ... a dating service?

"If you're through ..." I looked pointedly at JD

"I guess that's my cue to leave. I'll give you a call." JD smiled at Sage before nodding at me. "See you later, Garrett."

They did think this was a dating service. Well, they could just do it on their own time, not on mine.

"If you're ready...?" My voice directed at Sage sounded harsh even to my ears.

"Will your wife be there?" She looked a little dubious.

"What makes you think I'm married, and what difference does it make?"

"Well ..." She motioned in the direction of the house. "With the big house and all ..." Her voice trailed off.

"I'm not married, if that's what you're asking." I was getting fairly ticked off with the woman. She seemed capable of inciting my emotions with a word or a glance.

"Now if we have that out of the way, shall we go up to the house?"

She looked around. Everyone had already gone and we were the only ones left.

"If it's all the same to you, I'd rather hear what you have to say here."

I couldn't figure the woman out. She stood, arms wrapped around her middle as if to ward off my advances that weren't being offered. Her cute, worn out cowgirl hat was cocked at just the right angle to allow a few strands of her riotous red hair to fly loosely around her face.

What she did for old, worn-out jeans and a ratty t-shirt should be a crime.

I mentally shook myself out of the foolish thoughts. "Listen, if you think I have designs on your body, you're dead wrong."

Her shocked, sucked-in breath, caused my brows to lift and my eyes to roll. "Come on. Really?"

"I-I—"

"How about a compromise."

"Like what?" Sage looked more skittish than a newborn baby colt.

"You drive your"—I looked around for her vehicle and saw an old battered Chevy truck—"ah-vehicle up to the house. We'll sit on the porch and talk there. How does that sound? I think we have some unfinished business, especially if you decide to come back for the next class."

She stuck her hands in the back pockets of her jeans. "All right, but I can't stay long. I'm expected home soon."

I hadn't seen a wedding ring. But nowadays, that didn't mean anything. If she was, then why flirt with JD?

"It won't take but a few minutes." I struck off toward my truck, not waiting to see if she went to hers.

Once behind the wheel, for some reason, I didn't start mine until I heard her old Chevy spark to life. Once I did, I made a U-turn, heading for the house.

Why was I even bothering? What did it matter that she hadn't apologized?

For some reason, her actions *did* matter. People who thought they could get away with murder and then act as if everything was fine when it wasn't, galled me to no end. If she thought she could just waltz into my class after what happened between us, she had another thing coming. *Not happenin'.*

I parked out front so she'd know where to park, then got out and walked up to the porch. Without waiting on her, I sat in one of the wicker chairs.

When she parked and turned off the engine, her old jitney dieseled for a few seconds, then backfired, sounding like a gunshot blast. Still she sat, her hands gripping the wheel, looking out her front window at me. I began to wonder if she was just going to sit there and stare or back out and take off.

She let loose of the steering wheel and then opened the door. After jumping down from the truck, she headed in my direction, her boots kicking up little dust devils.

Sage was no longer a scared rabbit. She was a tigress on the prowl for meat for her cubs, and I was the one in her sights.

With a determined look, she stomped up the front steps, stopped at the chair opposite of me, then sat down. She pulled her hat off, laying it on the side table, before she proceeded to shake her head, dislodging a mass of long, curly red hair. Then she did that thing women do with their hands. She raked her thin, unmanicured fingers through her hair just before she swiped her hair back behind her ear.

With fascination, I watched the soft, silky strands bounce and then fall down around her shoulders and back. Apparently, she didn't realize how sensuous her actions were or how much they had affected me.

Get a grip. She's that spitfire from last week.

"Whew! That sure feels good." Her warm green eyes turned to look at me.

"Mr. McCasland, first off, I would like to apologize for my behavior last Saturday. I have no excuse for my conduct, even if there were mitigating circumstances."

She paused, changing her troubled expression to repentant. "Of course, none of them were your fault. I acted worse than any human being should have. My only excuse, I had gone to bed late and got up with the chickens, and was in less than a congenial mood. I hope you will forgive me."

How did she do that?

The woman had left me speechless.

Sage tapped her foot, giving me a puzzled look. "Well?"

"*Man!* You sure know how to catch a man off guard and slam it to him hard."

"And that means?" She wrinkled her brow, expecting an answer.

"Which means, yes, I'll have to forgive you. But I would like fair warning when you're going to do something so contrary to your nature."

"My nature?"

She was clearly confused, then it dawned on her what I meant.

"My nature?" Her lips compressed into a straight line as she crossed her arms, staring a hole through me. "What do you know about my nature? You know nothing about me."

"My experience, where you're concerned, last week and then again today, lets me know you are volatile and unpredictable. In fact, I would venture to guess at times your temper rivals your hair. And just like now, you have completely thrown me off my game with your apology."

"Game? What game? I'm not playing a game. If you don't want me to return to the class next time, I'll oblige you." She stood. "I didn't believe you could be so small minded. And I can't really say it's been a pleasure to know you, Mr. McCasland, because it hasn't. Good day." She turned to leave.

"Hey, wait just a minute." I caught her arm.

Giving me a deadly look, she jerked free. "Don't. Touch. Me."

"Sorry." I backed up, holding up my hands. "Listen, I think we got off to a bad start."

"Start? I don't think we were ever at the same gate."

I chuckled. "Yeah, you're probably right about that." I rammed my hand though my hair, and then rested my hand at the base of my neck, uncertain how to proceed.

"Listen, can we forget about last week? And maybe the last couple of minutes?"

I held out my hand, almost pleading for her to agree.

Again, she looked at me curiously. "And how do you suggest we do that?"

"I propose we start over, here and now, as if we'd never met."

She laughed. "I don't think you or I will ever forget last Saturday."

"True." I smiled, pouring on the old McCasland charm. "But we can at least be friends and forgive what took place." I held out my hand hoping she would take it in the way of a peace offering.

While looking at my hand, her brows scrunched together.

I was about to lower my arm to my side, disappointed she was so unwilling to yield.

She grabbed my palm and shook it, leaving me stunned and a little off kilter by the shock of her warm hand. I didn't want to feel anything for this little spitfire, but on some level she had conquered me, snatching away my ability to not be moved.

"All right. But I hope you won't think I'm always like that madwoman last week. I-I, well I have no excuse, except to say I'm sorry, and I hope you will forgive me."

"I do. And it's forgotten." Again, I grinned.

"Good." She hesitated, biting her lower lip. "Does this mean you won't mind if I come back for your next class?"

"You're more than welcome to attend. In fact, if you'd like, I could come over to your place, see what you're doing, and maybe suggest how to get an aquaponics system up and running."

Why in the world was I volunteering?

"Oh, I'm not sure that would be a good idea."

Instead of leaving it at that and being thankful, I had added one more chore to my already overloaded plate, I said, "Why? Is your husband against aquaponics?"

She smiled cocking one brow. "Is that your way of finding out if I'm married or not."

I laughed, feeling foolish. "Guilty as charged." Taking a breath, I knew better than to pursue this line of dialogue, yet, the words tumbled out. "Well, are you?"

"Married?"

"Yeah." I hoped with all my heart she'd say no.

"No. I have too many responsibilities to take on a husband, even if I found a likely candidate."

Relief poured over me.

Leave it alone. Say goodbye. "What kind of responsibilities, if not a husband?"

"Do you really want to hear this?

"Sure." On some level I wanted to know her better. Yet something within me said ... *get out while the gettin's good.*

She leaned her back up against the porch column, cocking her head to one side, studying me. I could see in her eyes the moment she decided to trust me.

"I take care of my grandmother. She lives with me, or rather, I live with her." She wrinkled her cute little nose. "She's my responsibility."

How bad could her life be? Don't ask. Sage is none of your concern.

"She practically raised me and I feel it my duty to take care of her since she's gotten older. My birth father skipped town when I was a baby. Gabby, that's my mother, left me in Grams' care while she flew around the world as a flight attendant, until she landed a wealthy husband. Several to be truthful."

"*Hmm.*" I was getting a whole lot more details than I bargained for. Yet, something about Sage drew me.

"Well, anyway," —she bandied her hand around like she was shooing a fly—"Gabby wants to put Grams in a rest home, and me to move to Dallas." She wants me to take a posh position with her husband's bank." She rolled her eyes. "Could you see me being diplomatic with rich clients?" She scoffed at the notion, making a ridiculous face. "*Not hardly.*"

I chuckled.

"The first one to cross me, I'd probably take his head off." She raised that one brow again, watching me, her face full of humor. "You saw up close and personal what I'm capable of doing to someone who just bumps into me."

"Yeah, I see your point." I chuckled.

She pushed away from the post.

"I've said enough for today. And Grams is expecting me back home. So I'd best be leaving."

She moved to the top step and stopped to look at me.

"I'm glad we had this little chat. And if I've interpreted your reaction correctly — you're not averse to me coming back. So, I'll see you in two weeks."

"And my offer still stands."

"Your offer?" She wrinkled her forehead.

"Yes, I'd be glad to come by your place and look at your layout. Maybe give you some suggestions."

"Let me think on it and get back to you. At this point, it's a pipedream of mine, nothing more."

"All right. But when you're ready, let me know. Have a good afternoon. See you next time."

She waved, walked down the remainder of the porch steps, then to her truck. Though her mannerisms, clothing, or the way she walked weren't seductive, there was a certain something about Sage that grabbed my attention and wouldn't let go. I couldn't take my eyes off of her.

When her truck started up with the first try and began to purr, I wondered what man kept the old wreck in such good running order? A mechanic, no doubt. Maybe a boyfriend, if she had one.

The thought of Sage and another man irritated me in ways I'd never felt before. Without a doubt, emotions like those would only lead me into quicksand.

Disgusted with my thoughts, I turned and went inside the house.

Woman trouble, especially in the form of a shapely, feisty redhead, was the last thing in the world I needed.

Chapter 6

Sage

All the way home, my thoughts strayed to Garrett McCasland. He was too appealing by half. Maybe I shouldn't attend anymore of his workshops. If I did, it could lead to trouble. And right now Grams and the farm needed me more.

I drove up the long drive and parked by the back door. Grams, her hand shielding her eyes, greeted me with a sweet smile.

"Well, did you have a good time?"

"Yes, I did." I gave Grams a hug. "Mmm, something sure smells good. Ah, let me guess." I closed my eyes, sniffing the aroma coming from the kitchen. "Stew."

Grams cackled. "Never could fool you." She moved back inside the service porch. "We had some of that pot roast left over. Stew just sounded good."

"It does." I sat down on the old parson's bench I'd found for a song at a yard sale a couple of years back. It was just the right size for the little mud room and for taking off my work boots.

I dropped my wallet and keys on the bench, and then removed my boots, storing them under the bench.

Grams held out a glass of iced tea. "Sit a spell and drink your tea. I want to hear all about the class."

"Not much too tell except I enjoyed it and ... you'll never guess who the instructor is. He's none other than the man I lit into last Saturday for dumping my lettuce."

"Oh, no. What did he say?"

I almost laughed at Grams' anxious face.

"Nothing at first, but then he asked to speak with me after everyone left. Once we were alone, I apologized for my behavior. I think we straightened it out, or at least I hope so. But as much as we need it, I'm giving back his lettuce money. I believe it's the right thing to do since the spill was my fault as much as his."

Grams nodded. "I agree. Don't you worry about a thing. We'll make do. Besides, the good Lord hasn't let us down yet." She patted my hand.

I swallowed some tea, allowing it to quench my parched throat. "I'm excited about what he's doing on his farm. And if I can, someday I plan to incorporate his ideas here. Of course, it'll be on a smaller scale *and* when we can afford it.

I stood and stretched. "Listen, if you don't mind, I'll tell you all about the class over dinner. I still have some chores left over from this morning. And then I need to take a bath before we eat."

"You go on. We'll have our chat later."

I pulled on my boots, went to reach for my hat, and knew exactly where I'd left it … at Garrett's. Grabbing my old standby, the brim a little more battered and with a few more holes, I slipped it on.

I headed out to the south pasture with the windows rolled down on ol' Betsy. The fresh, sweet smell of the outdoors filled my senses as the hypnotic ebb and flow of the tall green grass swayed like an ocean in the light breeze.

I drove along checking the fence. Thankfully, so far the barbed wire was in good shape and ready for moving the small herd on Monday. I'd take one more pass by the fence before moving the herd, but didn't figure I'd have any problems.

After making sure all my fencing was still in good order, I drove back to the barn, checked on the chicken feeder, ensuring it was full, then drove on up to the house. This time Sammy wasn't anywhere in sight. Probably out chasing some critter.

When I walked inside, I heard voices. Grams laughed and a man chuckled. I could hardly wait to get my boots off to see who it was since we seldom had visitors.

Entering the kitchen, my steps faltered.

Grams was bent over the open oven door. She was shoving a pan full of biscuits inside, next to the old blue enamel roaster full of stew.

Sitting at our table, as big as you please, was none other than Garrett McCasland. The sight of him in our little kitchen gave me a thrill but also unease.

Grams turned and caught me gawking.

"Look who came to visit." She smiled sweetly. "Your friend, Mr. McCasland."

He turned. I felt his discerning look take in my old hat, my colorful mismatched socks I refused to throw away, my dirty jeans, and my flyaway hair. I just hoped I didn't have dirt on my face. Come to think of it, the dirt might cover up the red from him catching me looking like a castaway.

"Call me Garrett." He spoke to Grams while continuing to stare at me with sparkling eyes.

"Why are you here?" Frankly, I didn't like that he was here and had caught me unaware. "How did you find me?"

"*Sage.*"

Grams' rebuke simmered me down some. But his chuckle stirred my temper again.

"Mr.-ah-Garrett brought your hat, thinking you might need it. Seems you left it at his house this afternoon." She gave me a look that said to watch my p's and q's.

He held it out to me, his right brow raised a notch.

"Thank you. But it wasn't necessary. I have other hats."

"So I noticed." His sparkling gaze made me want to smack him upside the head.

I would have snatched the old worn out hat from my head if I knew for certain my hair wouldn't look like a red bushy tumbleweed.

I took a deep breath to simmer down. "Thank you. I really appreciate you bringing it by." I tried to sound sincere.

His little know-all smile appeared again. "You're welcome."

"You go on up and take a shower. The biscuits will be done in twenty minutes. So hurry. Garrett's staying for dinner, and he won't want cold biscuits."

I wanted to say, I'll be down when I'm good and ready, and he'll just have to eat them however they come, but I knew better.

Rushing out of the room, I raced up the stairs, stripped off my clothes, and got into the shower. My heart was beating double time knowing Garrett was downstairs and would be eating at our old worn out table. What would he think?

Well, what's good enough for Grams and me will have to be good enough for him. Or he can just go home and eat at his own fancy table.

In record time, my hair was semi-dry and I was dressed in my best pair of jeans and my favorite turquoise top that set off my complexion. This time, I made sure my socks matched before traipsing down the stairs and into the kitchen.

Garrett sat at the table, laughing over something Grams had said.

I smiled until I realized Grams had been entertaining him with tales of my exploits when I was a child.

"There you are. I was just about to holler for you." Grams placed the pan of golden brown biscuits in the middle of the table on a hot plate, then covered them with a towel.

Garrett stared at me as if my clothes were on backwards.

Well, buster, what you see is what you get. And I'm not changing for any man, including you.

I went to the stove to carry the two bowls of steaming stew Grams had already dipped up. She carried the last one, setting it down at her place, leaving me the task of serving Garrett.

"Thank you." He smiled up at me.

I didn't return the smile. "You're welcome."

"Garrett, would you like to bless the food?"

"I'd be happy to."

Since I didn't know much about the man, his words shocked me.

He bowed his head and his deep baritone words sounded strange in our little kitchen where only Grams or I uttered prayers.

His voice sent chills through me, so much so, that I was unable to concentrate on the prayer.

"Help yourself." Grams lifted the towel, exposing fat, fluffy biscuits.

"Thanks, I believe I will." He grabbed one, sliced it open, then slathered butter over the whole thing. "Everything smells so good. I believe if I didn't already have an appetite, the smell alone would give me one."

Grams' cheeks turned rosy, her eyes lit up. "Well, there's plenty more, so eat up."

Silence settled over our little group while we all shoveled food into our mouths. Unlike Garrett, I had all but lost my appetite with him sitting so near. His bigger-than-life presence filled the kitchen, making it feel small, closed in, taking up all the air I breathed.

"What did you think of the class today?" His warm gaze fell on me.

When I didn't answer right away, he frowned.

I cleared my throat. "I enjoyed it very much. In fact, I'd love to do something like what you have done, but on a much smaller scale, of course."

Garrett wiped his mouth with his napkin, and rested his forearms on the edge of the table, studying me.

"You'd be surprised how a little operation can produce large amounts of produce, not to mention fish, if set up properly. And the learning curve's not bad. If you'd like, I can look at what you're doing now and make recommendations as to what you will need to match what you already have. Once you're up and running, you can even surpass what you're doing now."

I shrugged. "You're welcome to look over my field, but I'm afraid at the present time, moneywise, switching over is out of the question."

"I understand. However, once you have the means, I'll be more than happy to drop by and get you started."

"Sure. Thanks, but I can tell you now, no matter how much I would like to switch over, it might be years before I can afford to."

He returned to eating his stew.

"I know your folks." Grams smiled sweetly. "I wouldn't say intimately, but at least in passing. Your great-grandfather and my husband's father at one time had a co-op together."

"You don't say." Garrett looked surprised.

So did I.

"Land's sake, yes. Back then, there were three of them in the co-op. The McCaslands, the Andersons, and one more farm." Grams tapped her chin. "Let me see … oh, yes, the Petersons."

"I remember my dad mentioning something about Peterson. He was friends with the Peterson boys, I believe." Garrett laughed. "He said they used to get into all kinds of trouble.

"I can believe it. They had a passel of boys, six or seven." Grams laughed. "Seemed like they were always getting into mischief."

"Small world. Do you know what happened to the Petersons?" Garrett had polished off his bowl of stew. He grabbed another biscuit, slathered it with butter and then dipped his spoon into the wild berry jam I had put up last year.

"There was some kind of falling out between the three farms. I'm not sure what. But once that took place, it wasn't long before they dissolved their partnership." Grams cocked her head to one side, thinking.

"Unlike your family, the Andersons couldn't afford to automate when things began to change, and neither could the Petersons. A number of years later, the Petersons sold out and moved away." Grams waved her hand, glancing at me. "That was about the time old man Anderson passed on and your grandfather took over."

I knew my Grams didn't think much of my great-grandfather Anderson, but she would never say why.

Grams shook her head. "It was a well-known fact, that old man Anderson was a dandy around town and had an eye for the ladies. But all I ever saw was a crotchety old man that hated the world." Again she waved her hand. "But that's in the past." She tilted her head in thought. "When Slim, that's my husband, develop heart problems, well, he had to let the farm go to seed. He just couldn't keep it up."

Gram's patted my hand. "But now Sage is here. And the old Anderson blood has produced another farmer, regardless how small. She keeps us going with her little enterprise." She wiped her mouth looking embarrassed. "I've rattled on far too much. Would you like more stew? Biscuits?"

"No, ma'am. But it sure was good."

Grams stood and started clearing the table. "Well, I hope you saved room for dessert."

I scooted my chair back. Grams motioned me to stay seated.

"Entertain Garrett while I get the banana pudding." Grams looked back at him. "You will stay for dessert, won't you?"

"There's no way I'll pass up homemade banana pudding."

"Good. Visit with Sage while I dish up the bowls."

An awkward silence took place as I looked everywhere but at Garrett.

"I was wondering if you'd want to go into McKinney with me and catch a movie?"

"Well, I-ah-I"

"Sure she does." Grams' answered for me, her smile too bright.

I couldn't believe she was practically pushing me out the door with a virtual stranger. What did we know about him? *Nothing.*

"Great." He grinned as if it was settled and looked at his watch. "If we forgo the pudding, we can catch the seven o'clock. When I bring you home, maybe we can have dessert then, if that's not too late for you."

"I really should stay and help Grams."

"Go out and enjoy the evening with Garrett." The little matchmaker made a scoffing noise. "You've done enough today. I've got a book I want to finish. I'm only half way through it, and I'm anxious to see what happens." She smiled too sweetly. "I'll have your pudding waiting in the ice box for when you get back."

Seeing I wasn't getting out of going to the movies without looking unfriendly, I asked, "Are you sure?" I gave Grams my bug-eyes, hoping she'd get the hint and let me stay home.

"I am. Now go. You can tell me all about the movie tomorrow."

I turned to Garrett. "I need to run upstairs and get my jacket."

"I'll be right here, talking with Grams."

All the way up the stairs, even while I was digging out the money to pay Garrett back for the lettuce mishap, I wondered where he got off calling my grandmother Grams.

The man was getting way too familiar.

First showing up unannounced, and then staying for dinner, and now the movies.

Well, I have a good mind to march down those stairs and tell Mr. Self-Assured I'll be staying home, and he could just go off to the movies by himself.

Chapter 7

Garrett

What in the world was I thinking to invite Sage to a movie? I needed my head examined.

Sage waltzed back in the room, and I knew why. The woman was way too appealing for my own good and ... sanity. Normally, not attracted to redheads, this woman was heads above all the other women I'd known. If only her temperament matched her looks then we might be in business ... *not*.

I shook my head, smiling.

"Is something wrong?" Sage looked down at her clothes then back at me.

"No, I was just thinking how nice you look, is all."

A grin appeared. "Oh, is that all. Well then, thank you for the compliment."

"You do look pretty, dear." Grams was plainly proud of her granddaughter.

I, on the other hand, would have said gorgeous, because pretty didn't do her justice.

She walked over to Grams and gave her a hug.

"I won't be out late."

"Oh, don't worry about me. I'll be in bed asleep long before you get home. Y'all go out and have a good time." Grams folded her hands over her belly looking pretty pleased with herself. "And, Garrett, don't forget to eat the pudding before you head home, or at the very least take it home with you for tomorrow."

"Thanks, I'll do that." I glanced at Sage. "Are you ready?"

"As ready as I'll ever be." She looked a little dubious about our outing.

Grams walked us to the door and then waved us off.

"I hope she remembers to lock the door."

We were already heading down the drive. I applied the brakes. "Do you want to go back and check?"

Sage shook her head. "No, I don't know why I'm worried. She'll remember. She always does."

"You worry because you care."

"Yeah, I guess so. She's closer to me than my mother. And the fact that she's older and has no one to look out for her except me, causes me concern at times."

"What about your mother, won't she help?"

She made a scoffing sound. "Not hardly. Gabby, that's my mother, is a city person. She'd put Grams in a rest home if she had her way. She hates anything to do with country living and farming. In fact, she couldn't wait to leave the farm. And I couldn't think of anyplace I'd rather be."

She wrinkled her nose cute-like. "I guess you could say we are polar opposites."

"I lived with my grandparents up until I was ten. And then Gabby thought I should come live with her and her third husband. That lasted until my teen years." Raising her brows, she grinned. "She always said I was a handful.

Sage, unwanted by her mother, was drawing my compassion and digging inroads to emotions I didn't want to feel.

"Every summer while growing up, she would leave me with my grandparents, which suited me fine. In fact, I had a calendar and would mark off the days until I could be back on the farm. To me, the farm was a magical world with unlimited places to explore." She glanced out the side window.

Taking care of her grandmother, spoke volumes of the woman. The farm's poor condition and now knowing her predicament made me want to do something for her, but I didn't want that much commitment.

What possessed me to ask Sage out in the first place? We'd only seen each other three times if I counted the lettuce dump, and two times today.

"What has you smiling?"

Thrown off guard, I recovered quickly. "You have to promise you won't get mad."

"What are we, in grade school now?" She wrinkled her brow.

"No, ah ..."

She rolled her eyes. "Okay, I promise not to be mad at you, cross my heart, hope to die, stick a thousand needles in my eye. Give."

I chuckled. "Please, I hope you won't go to those extremes on my account."

Again she rolled her eyes. "Not hardly. *So?*"

"I was thinking about our first encounter." I glanced at her to see her reaction to me bringing up the fiasco.

"That was horrible. I can't believe I acted that way. But if you remember ..." She gave me a wide-eyed stare. "I did apologize."

"You did. And very nicely, I might add." I grinned. "In my mind, I could see booted legs in the air, a bushel of lettuce being flung about wildly, falling down around you, covering you like a blanket." I chuckled.

"For me, it was anything but funny." She pursed her lips.

"I'm sure. Still, when you sat up, wearing the lettuce, even spitting some of it out of your mouth, the only thing that kept me from laughing out loud was the wild and extremely heated look in your eyes. And then when that fiery temper of yours finally showed up, I didn't dare say a word. But I thought you were beautiful."

Sage stared at me strangely, probably judging if I was serious.

"Only someone crazy would find beauty in that mess." She glanced away and her shoulders began to shake.

I touched her arm. "I'm sorry, I didn't mean to upset you."

She turned to look at me and burst out laughing. "Don't be silly. I'm not upset."

"For a minute, you had me going."

"Do you know what I remember about last Saturday?"

"No, what?"

She took a deep breath. "I remember staring up into dark, concerned eyes. When I lit into you, your worry turned to confusion, before turning into anger." She angled her head to the side, staring at me. "Are you always that patient when someone flies off the handle and nearly tears your head off?"

Before answering, I took the onramp onto Hwy 75 heading into McKinney. "Now that all depends."

"On what?"

"Well, if it's one of my brothers, we're more apt to go outside and knock heads. I honestly felt horrible for knocking you down and then ruining your lettuce. That's why I left the money with Maude. She did give it to you, didn't she?"

Sage unzipped her little strappy purse, pulled out her small wallet. "Thanks for reminding me." She held out a fist full of bills. "This belongs to you."

"No, it doesn't. I ruined your sales last Saturday, and I always pay what I owe."

"You left far more than I would have ever made for the sale of my lettuce." She rolled the wad up and then stuck it down in my cup holder.

"Sage, put that back in your wallet."

"You don't want to see me throw another hissy fit, do you?" She grinned.

Shaking my head, I said, "No, thank you, ma'am. But—"

"What movie are you taking me to see?"

"Do you have a smart phone?"

She pursed her lips. "I may be a farmer, but I do live in the modern age."

Now I knew what made her so appealing ... her spunk and quick wit. And like my sister, she was never willing to let anyone get the better of her.

"Look up the theater and see what's showing."

Again, she unzipped her small purse, pulled out her cell phone and then started searching.

"*Well ...*" An impish grin appeared.

"Let me have it." I loved how she was so uninhibited around me. None of the first date jitters nonsense. As if we were old friends, nothing expected, except to enjoy one another's company. I hoped the evening stayed that way.

"Let's see ... one chick-flick, one sci-fi, and two burly-man movies. Oh, did I fail to mention one chick-flick?" She kept a straight face.

"I believe you covered it."

"Oh, well, first off—" She rattled off the names of each movie, then repeated the girly movie again.

"Why do I get the feeling you're angling for the chick-flick?"

"I tell you what, in one hand I hold the chick flick, in the other a burly-guy movie of your choice."

Cupping her hands together to make them round and hollow inside, she shook them up and down, as if she was shaking pieces of paper. We both knew she held nothing but air in her hands. She stopped, doubled up her fits. "Your choice … right or left."

Laughing, I asked, "And this is supposed to be fair? Not on your life. You'll cheat"

"You beat all I've ever seen. You're sure not a very trusting soul."

She gave a comical disgusted look. "Being an only child, I always thought I'd like an older brother, but you have completely changed my mind. Where's the trust? The chivalry? My faith in men has just sunk to an all-time low. I—"

"All right, enough. I'll play along. The left hand."

"Smart choice." Her eyes lit up as a grin tugged at her lips. "That my friend … is a chick flick." She stared straight ahead, a silly pleased look on her face. "It's a shame you didn't pick the right hand, it held the burly-man movie."

"You're impossible. And you *do* cheat."

"True, but I never said I didn't, now did I?" She showed me a face of innocence.

Pulling into the theater parking lot, I looked at the billboard, and then smiled. I got out and went around to open her door and help her down.

Walking inside, I wanted to touch her, even hold her hand. I resisted. Friends didn't do that kind of thing.

We stopped a little distance from the ticket booth.

"If you'll wait, I'll get our tickets."

"If you don't mind, I'll go to the ladies' room and meet you back here."

I waited until she was out of sight, then I walked up to the window grinning. I purchased two tickets for the mafia crime boss movie. Moving aside, I waited for Sage.

When she came toward me, my heart skipped a beat, my breath hitched. Then I noticed other attached and unattached males in the lobby following her with their lustful gaze. I wanted to rip out their eyes and tell them to find their own woman.

I shook my head to clear it of the caveman reaction. Somehow, this little spitfire was making inroads to my emotions, weaving a web around my heart. If I didn't put a cap on my emotions, she would have me trapped, unable to escape. And I knew exactly how I felt about that. *No way, no how.*

I was too young to be hogtied to a woman, regardless how appealing a package she might be.

"Is something wrong? You look like you have indigestion."

My face cleared. "No indigestion. Just working out a weighty problem."

"You want to tell me about it? I might be able to help. I'm pretty good at solving problems"

Honey, you are the problem.

I shook my head. "It's nothing. Would you like a cold drink and share a popcorn?"

"Sounds good."

"Wait here and I'll get it."

Within minutes I was back. "Are you ready to go in and get our seats?"

"Sure." She grabbed her drink before heading down the corridor in the direction of the chick flick.

"Sage."

She glanced back at me.

I nodded in the opposite direction. "It's this way."

She narrowed her eyes. "Just what movie did you purchase?"

"Since you were so fair in allowing me to pick the movie, I figured your real choice must be this one."

Looking up at the billing she started laughing and drawing attention.

"You cheated." She raised her brows. "But we think alike."

"How so?"

"This was my choice also. But I figured I'd see what you bought first, then go back and exchange them for this one."

I was plainly puzzled. Sage wasn't making sense.

"Garrett, it doesn't matter what kind of movie I watch, as long as it's not a dirty movie or a horror flick. That's where I draw the line."

Giving me an impish grin, she sashayed off, leaving me to watch her cute little swaying backside.

She glanced back at me over her shoulder, her brow wrinkled. "Are you coming or staying?"

"Coming."

I hurried to catch up, holding out our tickets to the young girl collecting them.

Without a thought as to whether I was behind her or not, Sage took off down the dark corridor before turning to continue up the stairs. A little above midway, she turned, moving down an aisle, walking to the middle. Without asking if these seats were okay, she sat down and placed her drink in her cup holder.

I followed suit. Our elbows bumped, causing some of the popcorn to spill.

"Sorry about that." I brushed off the pieces that landed on me, then balanced the tub on my lap.

Sage rescued the few kernels that fell on her lap, popping them into her mouth before giving me a look I could only describe as cute and sassy.

"Excuse me, but I think I was here first. The armrest belongs to me." She gave me a challenging hike of her brow.

"Your elbow wasn't there a second ago."

Seeing her determined stare, I said, "We could share."

"And how do you presume we do that. Your elbow is larger than mine and would leave me no room."

"Like this." I pulled her arm beneath mine, locking my fingers with hers.

"I guess that works."

As though holding my hand was perfectly natural and not world shattering, she relaxed and began looking at the previews shown on the screen. No first date jitters for her.

Sage was nothing like I had encountered with other dates, if this was a date. Usually, I had a struggle on my hands to keep the woman from latching on and not letting go while simpering and giggling, or saying, *whatever*. Usually, by the time the night was over, I was ready to dump them and run.

Not Sage. She might be unaffected by our close proximity. But me? I couldn't concentrate on anything but her. My fascination puzzled me. Other women, I could take them or leave them. Somehow Sage was different.

Oh, I was comfortable enough holding her small hand, yet the soft flowery scent she wore that filtered out the stench of the stale theater disturbed my peace.

She jerked and squeezed my hand while grimacing, startling me out of my thoughts.

"Sorry about that. And now you know why I don't like horror movies." She shivered. "Someone's always jumping out of the dark with an axe or something equally as bad, with a lot of blood and gore. *Oooo!*" She shivered again.

"That's why I'm here. To keep you safe."

"Yah, sure." She made a scoffing noise before looking back at the screen. "Oh, finally. Our movie is starting."

It wouldn't have mattered if the movie had been the best film in the world, my whole focus was on Sage.

She reached into the bucket of popcorn, pulled out a handful, her eyes on the screen. After devouring her handful, she took a drink of her coke. Never once glancing my way. Apparently, sitting close, holding hands, didn't have the least effect on her.

Unlike her, Sage held me captive. Her hand, her smell, how she felt up next to me, everything about the woman was driving me crazy. This redheaded spitfire came the closest in my thoughts for an ideal woman, except for her temper. And boy, did she have one.

Sage leaned in close. "What's funny? Certainly not this movie."

I whispered back, "Nothing, just thinking."

"If you're bored, we can leave."

"No, the movie's okay, for what it is."

"The plot's dumb and way too slow." She wrinkled her nose while reaching for another handful of popcorn.

I decided I'd better pay closer attention to the movie and less to Sage.

She was right. It was a dumb, boring movie. One I'd walk out on if Sage weren't with me.

When the bucket of popcorn was half empty, I'd seen enough.

Leaning in again, she nudged me. "This movie is terrible."

"My sentiments exactly."

"Let's leave?"

"Sounds good to me."

She slipped her arm from mine.

I wanted to pull it back, or at the very least hold her hand, but with my drink, the popcorn bucket, and stepping over feet, there was no way.

Out in the corridor, she turned to me. "You should really demand your money back. That was the worst movie I've seen in ages. Well, come to think of it, it's been ages since I've been to a movie, so I should say it's been eons since I've seen one this bad."

After dropping my drink container in the trash, I held out the popcorn. "Do you want any more of this?"

She shook her head, a devilish glint in her eyes. "We could sneak into the chick-flick."

"Really? I'm game if you are."

"Nawh. I'm all for leaving."

"Good." This time I did take her hand as we walked out of the theater to my truck.

I needed to date her again to see if we were a good match, or if tonight was a fluke.

From time to time, I had dated other women, but never seriously, and certainly none I liked as well as Sage. I couldn't put my finger on why except to say, she seemed to make my monotonous world spin on its axis and come alive in a way no one else had been able to do.

Chapter 8

Sage

"It's early, would you like to come in and eat your dessert?"

I wasn't sure why I'd asked him, except, I didn't want the evening to end, at least not yet. Maybe it was my innate curiosity about Garrett and how he seemed to turn my well-ordered life upside-down. Or maybe I was drawn to him because I hadn't had a date in so long.

"Sounds good to me, that is if you're not too tired."

"Me? Tired? No way." At least Garrett wasn't anxious to leave. Though we got off to an explosive start, I liked the man and wanted to learn more about him.

When we got out of the truck, he held my hand. Once again my blood raced through my veins. My emotions began flying all over the place.

Play it cool. He's just another man. I knew better.

Inside, I pulled out the pudding from the fridge and set it on the table. Garrett pulled out my chair, then sat down.

He took his first bite, and then closed his eyes. "Mmm-mmm. This has got to be some of the best banana pudding I've ever had. Your Grams sure knows how to cook."

I smiled knowing Grams would be flattered with his praise.

"Thanks. There's not much she doesn't cook well. But she'll be glad to know you liked it."

I took a few bites, too self-conscious of Garrett's presence to eat more. He seemed to affect me emotionally like none of the other guys I had known.

Leaning back, I watched Garrett devour his bowl of pudding, scraping the sides of the bowl, and all but licking it clean.

"There's more if you'd like some."

He gave a cute sheepish grin while patting his trim stomach. "Regardless how much I'd like to say yes, I have to say no. I'm too full."

"Something to drink — water, tea, coffee?"

"No, I'm fine."

"Shall we go into the living room then?" I stood, motioning in that direction, uncertain if he would want to stay longer.

"Sure, if I'm not keeping you up." He stood.

"Not in the least." I led him into the living room, turning on a lamp as I passed by. "Have a seat."

I sat on the couch and he followed me, sitting close enough to easily touch me. Feeling awkward and not sure how to open the conversation, I stared straight ahead, and then decided this was stupid. Garrett was a new friend, I needed to treat him like one.

Pulling the decorative pillow onto my lap, I twisted my body and raised my knee between us so that I could look at him. That was a mistake, I almost lost my train of thought.

"Tell me about your family. I know you have brothers because you said you would go out and knock heads. But how many are there, and do you have any sisters?"

He smiled, turning my insides to mush.

"I have three brothers and one precocious sister. Issy reminds me a lot of you."

"Me? How so?" I wanted to know everything there was to know about Garrett.

"Issy's a spitfire."

"Oh." That deflated my ego.

"Issy is beautiful, full of life, and always trying to fix me up with one of her girlfriends." He laughed, shaking his head. "It seems she would have learned by now."

"Learned what?"

"Her matchmaking will do no good. Like you, I have no plans of getting married anytime soon."

He had tossed my words back at me, which was a little disconcerting. "How old is Issy?"

"Let's see." His brows furrowed rather cute-like. "She's twenty-four, the baby of the family." He chuckled. "Being the only girl, I'm afraid we've spoiled her. We call her Princess or Miss Priss, which she hates, and is anything but. We give her a rough time when it comes to men. We all try to protect her from the wolves out there." He laughed.

"I'll introduce you to her one of these times."

So there was to be a next time. The thought excited me. "I'd love to meet her."

"What about your brothers? Are you close." I wondered if they were all like Garrett.

"I'd say so. However, we're complete opposites, except maybe for the youngest, Nick." He smiled. "He's a rancher and raises longhorns, so we have a lot in common. Justin, younger than me, is a policeman. Then there's Matt, the oldest and the lawyer in the family. All of us together do a good job of chasing Issy's guys off. Which, I might add, Issy hates."

"I would think so. If I were her and you guys were my brothers, I'd get even with you."

"Yup." He winked at me. "I knew it. You're just like Issy. For the last few months or so, she's been bringing one of her many friends home for family dinner. I think she's hoping we will find one we like and marry her. But that ain't about to happen.'"

I laughed. "I don't blame her one bit. Especially if she likes the guy and you run him off." Noticing my nervous habit of pulling the fringe on the pillow, I folded my hands on top of the pillow.

He glanced down at my hands, and then reached for my right hand, holding it in his. Turning my palm up, he ran his finger down my fingers and across my palm. The sensation was driving me crazy, not to mention it tickled like fire. When he glanced up into my eyes, he had a strange look I didn't recognize.

"For all the hard work you do around here, your hands are amazingly soft."

"Ah, thanks, I guess." His mannerisms and holding my hand was beginning to make me self-conscious again. "I don't do all that much."

His brow furrowed. "Oh, but you do. While I was waiting for you to come to the house earlier, Grams told me all that you take care of around the place. It's too much for a woman to handle on her own."

I snatched my hand back, perturbed that he sounded so much like my mother.

"You sound too much like Gabby, going on about how I should be sitting behind a desk and not tromping around in the fields chasing cattle and planting crops and getting old and wrinkled before my time."

Taking a breath, I did my best to calm my temper, but still the words spilled out. "I don't need you or my mother telling me how I should live my life. Women were emancipated in the early 1900s."

"I didn't mean it that way."

Standing, I said, "I find I suddenly have a headache. I'm sorry, but maybe you should leave."

He stood facing me. "Listen, I'm sorry. It wasn't that I didn't think you capable of doing the work. It's just—"

"Listen, before we both say words we don't mean and damage what I felt was turning into a beautiful friendship, why don't we say goodnight?"

Taking hold of my hand again, he frowned. "Sage, I'm truly sorry if I hurt your feelings. I didn't mean to. Will you forgive me?"

I couldn't look into his eyes. "Yes."

He lifted my chin with his knuckle, my eyes glued to his chest. His touch sent my emotions careening off into a precipice of doubt and confusion.

"Look at me, please."

His soft tone and the plea in his voice had me staring into his gorgeous blue eyes, filled with regret and something else I couldn't discern.

"I don't know where this—you and me—is leading, but like you I believe we have a beautiful, budding friendship I don't want to damage. I enjoy your company, and I would like more nights like tonight." He cracked a grin. "Well, except for"—he shrugged—"whatever got me into trouble a minute ago."

He cleared his throat, but it sounded more like a chuckle. "I promise to steer clear of the subject of women suffragettes."

I punched him on the arm.

"Ow."

"You deserved that and worse."

He lifted my hand, and then he kissed the back. The sensation of his lips on my skin sent vibes racing every which way through my body.

"Truce?"

Unable to speak, I barely got out, "Truce."

His eyes sparkled. "Friends?"

"Yeah." I nodded. "I would say we're friends."

He gave me a hug, which was totally unexpected and more like a brother would give a sister, then stood back. "Thanks, Sage. Even if we didn't have an auspicious beginning, and then I almost tanked it again tonight, I'm glad we have a do over and will become friends."

"Me too." I walked Garrett to the door. "Thanks for the movie."

He turned toward me. "Next time, you will definitely choose the movie. That way we might have better luck at finding a good one."

"Oh, so we're going to have another movie night?"

"Most certainly." He tweaked my nose. "Goodnight, and sweet dreams."

"Good night." I stood in the doorway and watched until he got into his truck and drove off.

If the erratic beating of my heart was any indication how I felt about Garrett, I was in deep trouble. The guy was beginning to mean more to me than a mere friend, which wasn't supposed to happen.

How could I go out with him and not fall for the guy? Deep inside, I knew if Garrett and I continued down this road, I wouldn't be able to keep my heart intact and from wanting so much more.

Chapter 9

Garrett

Friends, my foot!

The more I thought about last night with Sage, the more I knew, Sage as a friend would be like poking a snake with a stick. Eventually, the snake would rear up its head and strike someone — *me*.

Nope! Wasn't going there, regardless how tempting, or cute she might be. I'd have to keep my distance. Keep our relationship strictly business. I couldn't allow her green eyes to melt my resistance, or launch a raid on my heart.

I was the last to arrive at my parents' house for Sunday dinner. The only one living with my parents was Isobel, which was as it should be. However, all of us show up on Sunday. It's a family thing

Issy came running out the door, all smiles, launching herself into my arms, giving me a bear hug.

Oh, please, no, not another one of her friends invited to dinner.

She stepped back and gave me an odd stare. "Hey, handsome, why so glum? Aren't you glad to see me."

"Yes, I'm glad to see you. But if you remember, I just saw you at church."

"Not hardly. You waved from a distance. That's not seeing someone and saying *hey*." She gave a snort of disapproval.

"True, but I wasn't about to get hoodwinked into meeting another one of your friends." I wrinkled my brow. "You didn't bring one home for dinner, did you."

"No, silly."

"Isn't there a limit to how many girlfriends you have?"

She stuck out her tongue and then laughed. "I'm afraid not. If you remember, which I know you're getting old and forgetful —"

"I'll make you think old and forgetful." I grabbed her up and tickled her until she squealed *uncle.*

"Like I was saying, I was president of the debate team, homecoming queen, captain of cheer —"

"I get the picture."

"Oh, I failed to mention my sorority." Issy's impish grin appeared.

"Well, you can take me off the market. I've met someone."

Now why did I say that? I hardly knew Sage, and far as met, it was more like collided into her. And last night, well ...

"Garrett! You did?" She jumped up and down a couple of times, squealing, hugging me, then grabbing my arm. "I'm so excited. Who is she? Do I know her?"

She let go of me.

"Wait till I tell the folks. They'll be ecstatic." She started to take off toward the house.

I grabbed her arm, knowing she had taken *met someone* as involved with someone, which Sage and I weren't.

"Listen, we've only been out once. Nothing serious yet. But ... it could turn out to be more."

I figured if Sage got wind of what I'd told my sister, she'd go ballistic.

"Come on, tell me about her. What's her name? What does she look like? Where does she —"

"Whoa. Put a sock in it." My mind was working overtime to come up with answers without giving specifics or digging my hole any deeper than it already was.

"Like I said, we've only gone out once. I'm not ready to bring her home for dinner. If or when I am, you'll be the first to know all about her."

"Well, at least, give me a hint. Brunette, blonde?"

What could it hurt to give Issy at least one detail? "Redhead."

"Redhead!" Her incredulous look said she didn't believe me. "You've never dated a redhead before."

I smiled, remembering how Sage wasn't just any redhead. She was gorgeous, full of spunk, and fun to be around.

"Oh, no."

"What?" I wasn't sure what Issy thought she knew.

"You like her a lot, don't you?" Her dimples showed up. She stared at me oddly.

Up until this minute I hadn't given much thought about how much I liked Sage.

"I, ah—" Faced with the revelation that I was beginning to like Sage a little too much, I didn't know what to say.

"I knew it!" She did a victory punch. "I believe you're blushing."

"And I believe if you don't want more trouble than you can handle, you'd better keep your mouth shut to the family."

Smiling like she'd won a year's free shopping spree, she pulled her arm through mine and started walking toward the house. "Your secrets safe with me. She paused, giving me a smug smile. "That is if you give me her name."

"Issy, I'm not playing games with you. For the time being, this is between her and me. No one else."

"A name."

"You know … you can be one stubborn brat when you want to be."

"That's true." She wiggled her finger like she was trying to entice it out of me. "Give. I need a name, please."

"Sage."

"Like the bush?" Issy was intrigued.

"Yes. And that's all you get." I opened the door. "Now put a lid on it."

"Thanks."

Letting go of my arm, she began humming as she skipped into the living room and then on into the kitchen.

I figured Mom would know about Sage before I even got to the dinner table. This was one of those times I wished I was an only child.

"Hey, bro. What's up?" Justin scrutinized me as if I were a suspect. One thing about Justin, working as a cop, he didn't miss much—way too observant.

"Nothing's up. How'd your week go?" I figured I'd try to get him off the scent.

Justin shrugged. "Better than most. Fortunately, Primrose is quiet compared to Dallas, which I like."

"True." I moved on into the living room. "Matt." I nodded.

He grunted. We still weren't on good speaking terms since I'd quit his law firm and went full time with the farm. The fact that I would give up such a lucrative gig to become a farmer still stuck in his craw.

"Hey, Nick. How's the cattle doing?"

Nick pulled his gaze from the TV and nodded. "Doing good. I'll be having a calf sale by the end of the month. I got some good ones to offer if you know anyone in the market."

"Not off hand. But I'll keep it in mind."

"How'd your class go yesterday? Did many show?"

"I had eight show up, which wasn't bad." I smiled, remembering Sage.

With Nick owning a ranch of registered long horns and me into aquaponics farming, we always kept up with each other.

"What has you smiling?" Matt stared at me as if I was on the witness stand.

"He's got a gal, is why." Issy waltzed in the living room grinning from ear to ear.

I rolled my eyes and shook my head. "So much for keeping your mouth shut."

Really? I couldn't believe she was already running her mouth off. I figured I would at least be able to sit down to dinner before she said anything. *Women!*

My brothers and father stared at me.

"Well … are you going to tell us her name?" Dad turned off the TV—meaning, this discussion is important.

The room fell deathly silent. All eyes were on me. None of my brothers were married yet, and I was determined not to be the first one.

"Her name's Sage." Issy was practically beaming. She looked at Dad. "He wouldn't tell me her last name, but maybe he'll tell you."

I gave Issy a look of pure venom. I wanted to strangle her. "You just wait."

Her smug look said it all.

My father sat noncommittal, staring at me.

"Isobel is stretching the truth a little." Out of the corner of my eye, I saw Mom standing in the entry to the living and dining room.

"She's a redhead. Can you believe it?" Issy laughed.

"Isobel. That's enough." Mom's stern rebuke put a stop to Issy's antics. "Personally, I've always loved red hair."

Mom's defense of Sage made me feel a little better.

"Dinner is on the table getting cold. Shall we?" Her words got an immediate reaction.

I couldn't believe it. Thanks to dinner, I was getting a break. No more questions.

We all took our places. The smell was incredible, wetting my appetite.

Dad said the blessing, and as soon as the *Amen* was said, we began passing the food around the table.

"Is Sage from around here?"

Mom's quiet question meant she wanted an answer.

I cringed inside knowing one question would lead to another and then another, until I finally spilled my guts. I could either play twenty questions, or nip it in the bud by telling them all I wanted *them* to know.

"Yes. In fact, she lives not too far from my place. She has a small truck farm. I met her at the Chestnut Square market."

Nicholas started chuckling. "Don't tell me she's the spitfire redhead who gave you the shiner?"

I raised my brow, a little put out that Nick would bring up the incident.

"Well, is she?" Justin stared at me in disbelief.

"Yeah."

I took a bite of meat and chewed, the taste turning sour in my mouth.

My brothers and Issy started hooting and laughing and poking fun.

I wanted to pull them outside and give them something to laugh about but figured it wouldn't stop their teasing. It would just get worse.

"Boys." Dad's reprimand settled the motley crew, except for the shaking heads and huge grins.

"What's she like?" Justin split open a roll, smearing it with butter.

By the smirk he wore, I knew he wasn't through.

"We already know she has an explosive temper, but besides that ..."

Again, my siblings all busted out laughing

I bit the inside of my cheek wishing for once I'd stayed home instead of coming to Sunday dinner.

"One, she didn't purposely give me a black eye. That was an accident. Two, I wasn't watching where I was going when I ran into her and knocked her down. And three, I ruined her produce, so her temper was understandable."

"I don't quite remember it that way, do you guys?" Matt glanced around at his other two brothers who were shaking their head, laughing.

"Not hardly. The way I remember it, Garrett was hopping mad over the little redheaded hellcat." Nick chuckled.

"Boys." Dad gave them that look. "Let Garrett talk."

Though Dad had come to my rescue, by his look I knew he also wanted answers.

"You say she lives down the road from you. Which farm?"

"She lives with her grandmother about five miles down the road from me. Her name is Sage Anderson."

"Gabby's daughter?" Mom looked down the table at Dad.

"Yes, I believe that's her mother's name."

"She runs the Anderson farm now?" Dad's troubled face gave me pause.

What was going on here?

"Yes, she works a small portion of the farm by herself."

Both my parents processed the news, but not well. They appeared troubled.

"Her grandmother told me Sage's great-grandfather and ours ran a co-op of sorts, years back."

"That's true." Dad looked over the food on the table and then as if it was a revelation, he pointed to the basket of bread. "Matt, pass the rolls, please."

Everyone at the table turned quiet as if eating was one of the most important thing at the moment.

Something was terribly wrong, and it had everything to do with Sage's mother. I didn't have a clue what it might be. But I was sure going to find out—if not today, then soon.

Just one more reason, in a long list of reasons, why I should stay clear of Sage. *If I could.* Which appeared to be an impossible feat.

I needed to see her again to know where, if at all, our friendship was headed. Yet, friendship didn't seem to fit what I felt for Sage.

She fascinated me. She affected me like rain on dry, cracked earth. My main concern ... my thirst would never be quenched.

Chapter 10

Sage

A little apprehensive, yet wanting to look my best without being overly dressed, I stood before the mirror, studying my jeans and shirt.

Working around wet grow beds, with the possibility of getting my clothes ruined, I didn't want to wear anything too nice. I didn't have money to replace clothes as the result of vanity.

My junkies would have to do. It wasn't like I wanted to impress anyone.

My thoughts turned to Garrett, and I knew that was a lie.

Since the week after our movie, Garrett had dropped by a time or two with various excuses but hadn't asked me out again.

In fact, I hadn't laid eyes on him for a week now. He probably wasn't interested any longer, if he ever was to begin with.

Well, I wasn't interested in him either.

Maybe I shouldn't have refused JD when he called and asked me out last Saturday. He was a nice guy, and not bad looking. It was a shame JD didn't interest me. Maybe another look might not hurt.

Who was I fooling, my emotions were all tangled up with Garrett McCasland. JD didn't come anywhere close to measuring up to Garrett.

I glanced at the time, knowing I had only fifteen minutes to get to the class.

Dubious about going, I ignored my feelings, grabbed my wallet, then rushed down the stairs to the kitchen.

Grams was putting a pie in the oven. She glanced up smiling.

"So you're going to Garrett's class after all. Good. It's no slight on you that he hasn't come around this week. I'm sure the man's busy."

She wiped the back of her hand across her brow. "Tell him I baked a fresh apple pie, and he's welcome to come have a piece."

I shook my head. "Like you said. He's busy. He won't have time."

Moving over to where Grams stood, I gave her a hug. "You take it easy. And don't fuss over dinner. Leftovers sound good to me."

I stepped into the mudroom, to put on my boots.

"The class is only two hours today. But don't worry about fixing lunch. I'll fix a sandwich when I get back. Sybil Johnson is supposed to be there, and she loves to talk since we're the only two women attending."

One boot was acting a little stubborn, so I stood, stomping my foot a couple of times. It finally slipped into place.

"I have my cellphone, so call me if you need me. I'll see you later."

"You tell Garrett hello for me." She wiped her hands on her apron.

"I'll do that." I crammed my hat on my head, knowing Grams had put too much stock in a guy that wasn't interested in me the way she hoped he would be. Or for that matter, the way *I* wanted him to be.

That's life.

I learned years ago, not to set hopes on other people. Like with Garrett, it generally brought disappointment. Grams was the one constant in my life. She loved me unconditionally. And I loved her as much.

Because of my reticence to come, I was once again the last to arrive at the class.

Of course, Betsy once again let everyone know I was here. She backfired a couple of times, causing several people to turn and wave. Garrett wasn't one of them.

Glancing at my watch, I knew I wasn't late. There was at least another five minutes before class was supposed to begin. If he were perturbed it couldn't be because of me

I hopped out of the truck and then headed in the direction of the group.

Sybil motioned for me to come over by her, which I did.

She snagged my arm in hers. "Well, how have you been?" Sybil's dark eyes were bright with excitement. Apparently, she was anticipating some juicy gossip about Garrett and me, which I didn't have.

"Fine, and you?"

"Well, I'm just hunky-dory. And now that you're here, so is Garrett." She gave an un-lady-like snort. "I swear, if he looked once down that drive for you, he's looked a dozen times." Sybil got close to my ear. "That man is plum smitten with you."

"I don't think so. He probably thought I was hindering the class from starting."

"Not hardly."

"Well, since we are all finally here," Garrett paused and gave me a pointed look. "Let's go to the last hot house and I'll show you what I've added this week."

Sybil got close to my ear again. "See? What did I tell you? The man is smitten."

I chuckled, wishing it were so. "He's anything but. At least now I'm no longer costing him precious time."

"Think what you will. I've seen that look on men before. And Garrett's no different. He's singled you out. Mark my words." Sybil winked at me.

"Please, keep up."

Garrett didn't look at me, but he'd obviously aimed his remark in my direction.

This time, when Sybil nudged me, we both chuckled.

"Hey, how have you been?" JD Random walked up beside me with a grin bigger than a badger.

"I've been just fine, JD. How have you and Frank been doing? Started your aquaponic garden yet?"

"We're great. I've bought some of the plumbing items from Garrett, but nothing more. I have to buy the things as I get the extra cash, which is difficult to come by."

"I hear you." I nodded. "I'm having the same issue—lack of cash flow. Mine is a dream for one day down the road. Nothing now. Can't afford it."

"Yeah. Hey I was wondering—"

"Are you two going to talk or participate?" Garrett's stormy gaze was aimed at JD and me.

JD wrinkled his brow. "Participate."

"Good." Garrett studied me. "Then, JD, you want to lend me a hand with this?"

"Yes, sir." JD glanced at me. "I'll talk with you after the meetup."

"Sure."

"I could use your help now." Garrett's words were a little harsh, while he stood there, hands around some PVC pipe, watching the two of us.

"Here, let me help you with that." Ken stepped up and grabbed the other end of the PVC.

"Thanks." Garrett nodded at Ken. "JD, you and Frank, get the other two pieces and follow us. The rest of you keep up."

Sybil nudged me as JD walked off. "See. Garrett was none too happy about JD talking with you."

"Well, I don't know why not. He was just being friendly."

"Friendly, you say. *Humph.* I've seen friendly, and JD is anything but. If he can, he's going to give Garrett a run for his money."

"JD's just being nice, nothing more. And anyway, I'm not interested in JD."

Again Sybil latched onto my arm again. "Come on. We'd better catch up with the rest of them before Garrett comes back and begins to drag you by the hair of your head."

"Let him try."

Though I wanted to say plenty on the subject of the high and mighty Mr. Garrett McCasland, I didn't say a word. I just made sure I kept up with Sybil and the rest of our group, not wanting to give Garrett anything more to complain about.

Chapter 11

Garrett

I swear, that woman's yanking my chain. What does she mean, flirting with JD like that?

First, she shows up late—well maybe not late, but after everyone else has arrived. She stands there laughing and talking with Sybil, without so much as a look or *hi* in my direction, while all this time I've been waiting for her to get here.

And then, as if on cue, along comes JD sidling up next to Sage. Seeing them together was worse than a wasp sticking his stinger under my skin and giving me a double shot of its nasty espresso venom. Then to add insult to injury, Sage goes all smiley over JD.

What did I care.

I was having difficulty concentrating, and Sage was the culprit. I didn't need this kind of distraction today, or for that fact, anytime.

Women were nothing but trouble, specifically Sage Anderson.

For the rest of the class, I made sure I kept JD busy and away from Sage.

"I believe you have a good foundation for setting up your aquaponics' farm. However, if you have any questions, don't hesitate to contact me. I've set some handouts on the table over there. It's been a real pleasure. Keep in touch and let me know how your system is working."

Ken and a couple of the other guys caught me and began asking questions. Without being obvious, I tried to keep my eyes on Sage. I relaxed when I saw she was talking with Sybil and JD wasn't anywhere near her.

I wrote down some measurements for Ken, and then answered a couple more questions for Frank and one of the other guys. It dawned on me, JD wasn't standing here with his brother any longer.

Glancing around, I spotted JD, who was once again talking and laughing with Sage and Sybil. I wanted to go over there and pound the guy into the ground.

Being controlled by my emotions was plain stupid. I held my temper and allowed the other men to finish asking their questions, to which I gave short answers.

"Listen, if you don't mind, I need to catch Sage before she leaves and-ah-give her some information. You have my number and email. Contact me if you have more questions."

"I'll walk with you since I see Sybil is with Sage."

I grunted, then remembered my manners. "Sure."

"Ah, and I see there's our JD. Like a bee to nectar, he seems drawn to Sage." Ken chuckled.

"He's not my JD," I mumbled under my breath, but not soft enough.

Ken slapped his leg and brayed like a donkey at my expense.

I shook my head, smiling.

"She's a beauty, isn't she?"

"Who?" I looked at him as if he'd gone nuts.

Ken laughed, "I would say my wife, but she's taken." He nodded at Sage. "I don't believe you can find anyone better if you were to hear my wife talk."

"Listen, please keep this between the two of us."

The man gave me an approving look. "Will do. But if I were you, I wouldn't wait too long to speak up."

"Hey, hon, you ready to go get something to eat?" Ken walked up and gave Sybil a hug.

She smiled at her husband. "Sure, if you're ready."

"I am." Ken nodded at JD. "Keep in touch. Let me know how your brother and you are getting along with your system."

"Will do."

"And you do the same." Sybil hugged Sage. "Let me hear from you. And one day soon, let's have lunch."

"Thanks, Sybil, I'd like that."

"Speaking of lunch ..." JD looked at Sage longingly. "Would you like to go get a bite to eat? My treat."

JD asking Sage to lunch made my stomach burn like I'd swallowed acid. I wanted to plow the guy six feet under for looking at her. He didn't have a right. She was ...

Hold that thought. She's not yours. So, back off. Way, way off.

Instead of telling JD she couldn't go, I bit the inside of my jaw so hard, I thought it would bleed. I backed up a foot or two and prayed Sage wouldn't accept his invitation.

"Thank you so much for the invite, JD, but I really need to get home. My grandmother is expecting me. Maybe another time."

Another time, my foot. I was steaming mad to think Sage might go out with JD. She didn't have a right.

Oh, but she did.

"All right then. I'll give you a call."

Sage started off toward her truck.

"If you've got a minute, Sage, I'd like to speak to you." I gave JD a look, that if he didn't understand my meaning, I just might have to explain it to him.

When JD walked away, I didn't know what I wanted to say to Sage. So I stood there and looked at her. I wanted to snatch her up and carry her off before JD or anyone else equally determined tried to steal her away.

"Well?" Those green eyes of Sage's snapped and sparkled. "What did you need to speak to me about?"

"Ah-yeah, how is Grams?" I felt stupider than Job's turkey standing in a field of holiday hunters.

She blinked, and for that one nanosecond I felt desperate. I wanted her to smile at me, talk to me, or at the very least, acknowledge me as she had JD.

She wrinkled her brow. "Grams seemed a little under the weather when I left to come here."

"Sorry to hear that."

Sage became introspective, raising her brow. "She said to tell you hi, and to come by and get a piece of pie soon. In fact, she was putting one in the oven when I left."

"Sure sounds good. Is that an invite?"

"I believe it was." Sage cocked her head, staring at me through hooded eyes. "What exactly did you want to speak to me about?"

"I want you to know if you ever need help getting an aquaponics system in place, give me a call. In fact, I have some left over parts I'm giving you to get started."

"Thanks, Garrett, I appreciate it." She smiled but it didn't quite reach her eyes. "At the moment, I don't see my way clear. If I ever get the money, I'll give you a call." She grimaced. "I can see the merits of aquaponics, and it would sure make my life easier."

When I didn't say anything more, she shrugged. "You're welcome to come by later for some pie."

"Sure. And tell Grams hi, and thanks for the invite."

"I will." She waved, heading for her truck. "Later."

"Yeah, later."

I took off my hat, ran my hand through my hair. Like a moonstruck kid, I couldn't take my eyes off her. I loved everything about her. Her feistiness, her spunk, the way her temper ignited, making her eyes sparkle like emeralds in a sea of glass.

I had to make a move or lose her. But today wasn't the day. It was too soon.

Chapter 12

Sage

"I'm ready to leave, Grams." I walked in the kitchen, cash box in hand.

"I'll be praying you sell out today." Grams wiped a strand of gray hair from her face while sitting at the kitchen table.

She looked a little too pale, which worried me. Yet, I didn't have anyone I could call to come look in on her while I was gone ... except for Garrett. I wouldn't call him.

If only I had friends in Primrose, my life would be much simpler. Working from sun up to sun down and beyond wasn't conducive for making and keeping friends. Thanks to Gabby hauling me off to Houston to finish high school, and then on to college, all my friends weren't from around here.

Sybil. No, Grams hadn't met her yet, only heard about her from me. She'd be uncomfortable with a stranger in the house.

"Grams, are you sure you're feeling okay? You look a little peaked."

"I didn't rest well last night, but other than that I'm fine." Her smile was as sweet as ever.

Her lack of rest worried me. Yet, I knew older people sometimes have sleepless nights, and then slept during the day. Maybe this was Grams' case.

"Listen, I don't want you doing anything while I'm gone. Get one of your books and sit in the recliner. Read or get some rest. And please don't worry about supper. I want your opinion on this new recipe that I want to try out. So, I'll be cooking when I get home."

I really didn't have a recipe, but I would have one by the time I got back this afternoon. Someone at the market was always sharing recipes.

"What're you thinkin'? Garrett will drop by later today and you'll show off your cooking skills?" Grams laughed, putting a little color in her cheeks.

"Nawh. Just you and me."

I hadn't heard from Garrett since last Saturday when he came by for a piece of pie. He called once, but that was to see how Grams was feeling. And since the meetup was over, I didn't have an excuse to go by and see him.

I wasn't about to destroy Grams' hopes by telling her he might drop by, when he probably wouldn't.

Hugging Grams up close, she felt so frail in my arms. How old was she? Eighty-nine? Too old to be fussing over dinner or a house. Maybe I could find a part-time job so I could hire someone to help either around the house or the farm. That way it would make Grams' life a little easier. But then what would that do? She'd still cook and fuss about the house.

Grams walked me out to the back porch and then leaned against the railing.

She shooed me off. "You go on now. And don't you be a worrying about me. I'll be fine. You just have a good day." Grams looked drawn, her shoulders a bit slumped.

"I should be back no later than two."

"I'll see you then."

"Make sure you get some rest."

She waved me off, then turned to enter the house.

Driving a little slower than usual, I watched from my rearview mirror to make sure Grams made it back inside. She did. Yet, I felt awful having to go off and leave her.

Maybe the job with my stepfather, Robert, might be a good idea after all. I could rent a small house or apartment in Dallas. Grams could still live with me. That way, I'd have a better income, with no worries or stress for either Grams or me.

The idea of moving into town didn't set well with me. But if it would make life easier on Grams, I'd do whatever was best for her.

My drive took me past Garrett's farm. My gaze strayed to his beautiful house. There was no sign of Garrett's truck, but that didn't mean anything. He could be in the back working in one of his greenhouses.

How many times had I driven past his place without knowing he lived there?

I shouldn't have been, but I was a little disappointed when Garrett didn't come by or ask me out. Men friends were different than women friends. I realized that. Women called and checked up on one another. Men ... well, they didn't, except on occasion.

No doubt, I wouldn't hear from Garrett again, unless I ran across him in town or passed him on the road. Which is how it should be. *Distant friends.*

I pulled into a parking space at the market and then jumped out of the truck to untie the tarps on the backend.

Someone came up behind and took the rope from my hands.

"Here, let me get that."

I nearly fell off the truck running board.

"Garrett? What are you doing here?" I turned around.

He was too close. His gleaming smile snatched the breath from my chest as the soft smell of sandalwood filled my lungs. His hands surrounded my waist. He lifted me from the sideboard, then gently set me on the ground.

I wasn't sure if my legs would hold me up, I was that close to melting from his touch. Especially, with him staring at me like he couldn't get enough of me stored up for those long dry spells.

Garrett was too good-looking to keep my heart in check. The dark blue jeans fit him to perfection, and his blue button-down shirt set off his gorgeous blue eyes, that at the moment, were glued on me and making me very self-conscious.

"Are you here to sell your produce at the market?"

His eyes sparkled as he skillfully took over the chore of untying the stubborn knot.

"No. I have a contract for my produce with one of the restaurants in downtown McKinney. I just dropped it off a few minutes ago."

Fortunately, he took over the job of untying the other knots, giving me time to get myself under control, if that were possible. I was a quivering mess around him.

"Since I was in the area, I thought I'd come by and see if I could lend a hand." He took extra care pulling the tarp off my vegetables.

"Here." He held one end of the tarp out toward me. "You want to help fold this."

Pulling myself from my stupor, I grabbed one end. "You don't have to do this."

He shrugged, smiling. "I know, but we're friends, aren't we? That's what friends do. And … I wanted to see you." His grin was anything but innocent.

"Oh." Excited that he wanted to see me, I nervously pulled on the tarp.

In no time at all, the thing was folded and inside my truck. Garrett pulled out a table and began toting it up the hill where we'd first met.

My face heated remembering our disastrous first meeting.

Was he remembering it too?

Grabbing a bushel of vegetables, I followed him. He set the table up before heading back to my truck for more stuff.

Maude's booth was already set up, but empty, thankfully. Otherwise, there'd be no end of what she might say on the matter of Garrett helping me.

We worked well together, and had my things unloaded and set up in no time.

Maude came from the opposite direction. When she saw Garrett, her grin got bigger than a wedge of watermelon.

She gave me an exaggerated wink. "Well, well. Garrett, isn't it?"

"Yes, ma'am. Nice to see you again, Maude."

"All I got to say to you, young man, is you must be a glutton for punishment." Maude cackled while she walked around behind her table and sat down.

"No ma'am. I believe Sage and I have worked out an arrangement." He winked at me. "I don't knock her down when she's carrying lettuce, and she won't spit lettuce in my face."

Maude slapped her lap, chuckling. "I told Sage you were one of the good ones. And I wasn't wrong."

"Why, thank you." He glanced at me. "I hope to convince Sage over to your way of thinking."

Talk about embarrassing. I looked down at my table, rearranging a jar that didn't need to be, wishing this conversation over and done with.

"Oh, you're a quick one. No one's gonna take you for a ride."

"I hope not." He turned to me. "Listen, I've got some errands to run. When do you close up?"

"Noon." I was plainly puzzled. Surely, he wasn't thinking about coming back.

"All right then." He tipped his hat at Maude. "It's good to see you again. And as I mentioned last time, your tomatoes are beautiful, just like you."

"Ah, you go on now." Maude shooed him with her hand. "Your flattery will get you a whole lot of nothin'."

He laughed. "Ladies, it's been a pleasure."

Garrett was gone before I could tell him bye. I watched his strong, impressive form saunter down the hill, wishing I could go with him.

Now, where did that foolish thought come from?"

"You got yourself a good one there. Even after you lit into him like a banty hen, he still came around. I don't know how you did it, but don't you dare chase this one off. I like the man. He's a keeper."

A person came up to Maude's booth, making it impossible to tell her we were just friends and nothing more.

We were swamped with customers all morning long, both new ones and regulars. Maude and I had little chance to further our conversation.

It seemed like I'd barely set up before I saw that it was noon. Most of my vegetables were gone, over half of my honey, and I had only a few home-canned goods left.

I turned to get the box to pack up.

"Your man's here."

I looked over to Maude, wondering what she meant.

"My man?"

She grinned and nodded, her gaze hooked on something across the way. "He's like a bee to nectar. I'd say that man's got it bad."

When I glanced across from us, I saw Garrett, standing, talking to one of the vendors.

I turned to Maude and hissed, "Maude, don't you dare embarrass me. Garrett is nothing more than a friend." The last I mumbled under my breath.

"*Humph!* That guy has love written all over him."

"Maude! Please!" I ground out through my teeth. "He might hear you."

My face flaming, I began grabbing and shoving stuff every which way into boxes, trying to have everything packed before Maude did something harebrained, like motion Garrett over to my table.

"Hand me a box. I'll help you pack."

Still too disconcerted that Maude might say or do something to embarrass Garrett or me, I didn't look up. "Thanks, Garrett, but I can do this. You helped enough this morning, I don't want to impose."

Stilling my hand, Garrett nudged my chin up to look at him. "Sage, what's going on?"

"Nothing." I lowered my eyelids, unable to look him in the eyes.

"I thought you understood, I'd be back to help you pack."

"Oh." I couldn't think of anything else to say.

"This isn't like you. Where's that straight-forward, fun-lovin' gal gone?"

This time, I did look at him. All I saw was good-natured friendliness.

I could do friendliness.

"Thanks, I'll accept your help." I handed him a box. "Put what's left of the vegetables in this one."

"Okay." He whistled. "Man, do you always do this good? You've just about sold out of everything you brought."

My heart glowed with his praise. I smiled. "Not always, but most the time, if we're not rained out."

"Well, all I've got to say is, *wow!*"

His smile and compliment made the sunshine brighter. His thoughtfulness touched me in ways no one had in a long time. He was definitely a good man. And my heart was making more out of Garrett's overture than was meant to be.

Now how do I keep Garrett as a friend, when my heart wants so much more?

Accept it, Sage, you can't make someone love you.

Chapter 13

Garrett

Something was up with Sage. She was less than enthusiastic when I said I'd follow her home to help her unpack. And ... she wouldn't look me in the eyes.

Maybe she was upset because I hadn't asked her out again. And I hadn't been around to see her since last Saturday.

I wanted to. Even picked up the phone several times, but I talked myself out of it. I wasn't sure if I was ready for that next step—crossing that invisible line to love—especially when I didn't' know how she felt about me.

She motioned for me to park beside her.

I rolled down my window.

"Let me check on Grams, then I'll unload in the barn."

None too happy to be relegated to stay in the truck, I thumped my thumbs on the steering wheel, looking around.

The siding needed a good scraping and a couple coats of paint, but other than that, the house and barn looked to be in fair condition. For one small woman looking after a place this size, Sage did a remarkable job.

"Garrett!" Sage stood on the porch, tears were streaming down her face.

I got to her as fast as I could.

She gripped my shirt in desperation. "Help me, please. I can't wake Grams."

Her sobs tore at me.

She opened the door and ran back into the house.

"Have you called 9-1-1?" I was pulling my cell out of my pocket.

"No."

I dialed 9-1-1 while following Sage.

"9-1-1. What is your emergency?"

"I need a paramedic." Inside, I followed the sound of Sage pleading with her grandmother to wake up. I gave the operator Sage's address, and all the information I knew and then hung up.

When I walked into the living room, Grams was slumped over in the recliner, unresponsive. Sage turned pleading eyes to me. I had never felt so helpless in all my life as I did at that moment.

"Does she have a pulse?" My heart twisted when I saw Sage's scared gaze.

"Barely."

"I've called for an ambulance. They should be here soon." I moved over beside Sage and lifted Grams' hand, feeling for a pulse, but couldn't find one. I put my ear to her face hoping to feel her breath. *Nothing.*

Next, I put my head to her chest. I wasn't sure if I heard a heartbeat or not.

"Sage, I need to lay her on the floor and start CPR until the paramedics get here."

"Please." She grabbed an afghan off the sofa, throwing it out on the floor.

Once I had Grams' on the floor, I checked her mouth to ensure nothing was obstructing her passageway. I didn't see anything.

In my head, I began to sing "Staying Alive" while I started the chest compressions.

Grabbing another wrap from the chair, Sage put it over Grams, then knelt holding her hand, feeling for a pulse.

It seemed like an eternity before I heard the siren, faint at first, and then loud enough to know it was outside the back door.

"Let them in."

Sage got off the floor and ran to the back door. It wasn't too many seconds before two men followed Sage into the living room.

One of the men knelt across from me. "Thanks, I'll take it from here."

I stood up, then moved back, allowing the medics room to work.

Sage came over and stood by my side. I slipped my arm around her waist, pulling her close, comforting her as best I could. Tears slipped down her face, her body shook with silent sobs. She was so fragile, so frightened, and so alone.

I felt useless.

The medics asked a few questions which Sage answered. They lifted Grams up on the gurney, started an IV then hooked her up to the monitoring system.

"Is she ..." Sage didn't finish.

"At the moment, she's holding her own." The man speaking to Sage was about my age. "We're taking her to Baylor in McKinney."

"Thanks, we'll follow you," I spoke for Sage and myself.

The men strapped Grams in and began to move her through the house.

"You've done so much, Garrett. I don't know what I would have done if you hadn't been here. Thank you. I'll follow the ambulance." She had hurried from the living room to the mudroom to slip her boots on.

"I'm not going anywhere. I'm driving you to the hospital."

"I can't let you do that." Sage shook her head, stepping back. "I'll need my truck since I don't know how long it'll take."

"Listen, I'm not taking no for an answer. You're in no state of mind to drive. I'll take you in my truck and stay with you until we know what's going on with your grandmother. One of my brothers can drive your truck to the hospital if need be."

"That's too big of an imposition." She grabbed her purse and keys.

"Sage, look at me."

When she did I knew she was too upset to drive.

"It's settled. You're riding with me, even if I have to hogtie you to the seat of my truck."

I heard a small burble of laughter, glad I could bring some sunshine on such a dark day.

"All right. On the way, I'll call Gabby and let her know about Grams. I'm not sure she'll come, but I have to let her know."

What type of woman wouldn't come to visit her own mother in the hospital?

Thankfully, Sage wasn't anything like her mother.

Once in the truck, I took out after the ambulance, wondering what Sage would do if her grandmother didn't pull through. Saying a silent prayer for Grams, I had an intuition only a miracle would bring Grams through the night.

Sage pulled out her cell phone.

I didn't want to eavesdrop, but it was hard not to.

"Hi, Gabriella Stanton, please. This is Sage Anderson." Sage turned her head to look out the side window.

What was up with Sage's mother not wanting Sage known as her daughter. What kind of woman would do that?

"Hi, Gabby. It's me. Grams' is on her way to Baylor in McKinney." There was a pause. "No, I don't know what happened. She was unconscious when I got home from the market." Another pause. "Yes, I'll call you and let you know as soon as I find out. Yes. All right. Bye." The phone lay in her lap as she wiped her face.

By the sound of it, Gabby wasn't too interested in beating a path to the hospital.

Sage's shoulders sagged and then began to shake.

I reached over and took hold of her hand. "I'm so sorry. I wish there was something I could do."

My words sounded so lame. I wanted to stop my truck and take her into my arms and absorb all the hurt but knew that was impossible.

"I'm just so glad you followed me home. I don't know what I would have done without you."

"Hey, listen, I'm more than happy to be there for you and Grams."

Sage fell silent. I figured she needed time to process the possibility Grams could die. I prayed she wouldn't.

The trip to Baylor was quick, especially since I'd caught up with the ambulance and we were traveling behind them well above posted speeds.

Along the way, I watched for Justin, but the old adage *where's a cop when you need one* was in full force and effect. I figured I'd give him a call once I got to the hospital and knew about Grams. Hopefully, he'd be able to take me back to Sage's to jockey her truck to Baylor.

We were ushered into a waiting room, told where the cafeteria could be found, and that they would come get us once they were through working with Grams. I led Sage over to a couch, and then pulled her down beside me, my arm nestling her into my side.

She rested her head on my chest and softly cried until she was spent. Pulling back, she wiped at my shirt.

"I'm sorry. I'm afraid I made a mess out of your shirt. But thanks for your comfort." She gave me a watery smile.

"Hey, you can use my shoulder or shirt anytime." I wanted to say more but figured this was neither the time nor place. Something about holding Sage in my arms, comforting her, reinforced the thought there was so much more going on between us than mere friendship.

I prayed when this was all over, she would feel the same.

We sat in that little room well over two hours. During which time, I went downstairs and brought up sandwiches and a couple of drinks. Sage ate about half of hers, if that much.

She called her mother once to let her know they were still working on her grandmother. Not once did Gabby call to check in on her own mother.

A nurse came into the room and looked in our direction. Since we were the only ones sitting in the room, I figured she was looking for us.

"Are you the Anderson family?"

Well, I wasn't family, but she didn't need to know any better.

"Yes." I nodded at her.

"If you'll come with me, the doctor would like to speak with you."

I took Sage by the hand as we followed the woman down a maze of halls. She showed us into a room with generic pictures, chairs, tables and lamps, and Kleenex boxes.

"Please have a seat, the doctor will be with you shortly."

The door shut quietly behind the nurse, yet it sounded like the door closing to a tomb. Sage rubbed her arms as if to ward off the cold. Glancing up at me, she gave me a weak smile. Once again, I put my arm around her waist, allowing her to lean on me.

When the door opened, Sage pulled away.

"Hi, I'm Dr. Henshaw. I understand you are Mrs. Anderson's granddaughter?"

"Yes, I'm Sage Anderson, and this is my good friend Garrett McCasland."

"Sage, I'm sorry to report that your grandmother passed away a few minutes ago."

"No."

Sage's weak mew of a cry tore at my heart. She leaned into me, her silent sobs shaking her body. I held her in the circle of my arms praying the hurt away but knew it was something she had to face.

"What happened?" I wanted to know as much as I knew Sage needed to know.

"Mrs. Anderson suffered a heart attack. Her heart was just too weak."

I continued to hold Sage close.

"There was just the two of us." Sage looked at the doctor. "It was my fault. She worked too hard cooking and cleaning while I ran the farm. She was eighty-nine. I should have known better." Sage's hand muffled her words.

Taking the blame for her grandmother's death made me want to fight back, but with who?

Dr. Henshaw shook her head. "If anything, the benefits she received from her working around the house helped to prolong her life. Her death would have come much sooner if she'd sat around doing nothing." She held out a card. "This is my number. If you have any questions, please don't hesitate to call."

"Thank you." Sage shook the Doctor's hand and then I did.

"Thanks for all you did."

The doctor nodded, and then quietly left the room.

Sage sat down, her head bowed, hands folded.

The need to hold her until the pain went away was overpowering. I slipped my arm around her shoulders. Even if I couldn't erase the pain, I could maybe ease it some by letting her know I cared and was here for her.

She leaned into me, her arm around my waist, head on my chest. At that moment, I knew I cared for Sage far more than I could have ever imagined. She meant more to me than any woman I had ever known.

How did my heart get caught up so quickly?

One day the object of a lettuce dump with Sage taking an inch off my hide, and definitely my pride. Now holding her in my arms, doing my best to console her when I didn't know how.

I'd fallen hard for this beautiful redhead. My only worry, I didn't know how Sage felt about me. And now with Grams' death, I knew it wasn't the proper time to speak. Yet, if she didn't return my feelings, I would experience a grief like none I'd never known before.

She looked up at me, her eyes red and puffy, grief written on her face.

"Garrett, how will I live without her? Grams was my constant. It has only been the last few years that I tried to give back to her for what she's given to me. Now she's gone."

"You're not in this alone, Sage. I'm not going anywhere. I'll help you with whatever you need me to do."

She sniffled, pulling back, looking down at her hands.

I pushed a strand of hair from her face and then held out the Kleenex box, waiting until she'd wiped the tears from her cheek and blew her nose.

"Thanks, Garrett. You're such a good friend." She stood, the sadness a part of her. "I'd like to go home now."

Sage was one of the strongest women I knew. And she wouldn't want my pity, nor for the time being, even my love. Yet, I wasn't going to let her go through something this tragic without being by her side to show her how much I cared.

Chapter 14

Sage

The ride from the hospital was quiet, except for my occasional sniffle and the call to Gabby.

She cried a little.

I cried more.

Garrett held my hand doing his best to infuse comfort.

"Would you like me to come out there?"

Why Gabby thought I needed her *now* was a mystery.

"Not especially. My friend, Garrett, is with me."

He squeezed my hand, nodding.

I hoped he didn't mind that I used him as a scapegoat, but once I got off the phone, I'd explain my reasoning.

"Garrett? I've never heard you mention this Garrett before. Do I know him?"

"No, you don't."

"Well, I hope this Garrett guy is not some country hick without two nickels to his name. You can do better, particularly, since you will be moving back into town now."

I ignored her jab and also her foregone conclusion that I was leaving the farm and moving to Dallas. I wasn't. And I wasn't having this conversation, especially with Garrett within earshot.

"I'll make the arrangements for Grams' funeral and call you when they're completed."

Garrett wrinkled his brow, probably wondering what Gabby was saying on the other end to make me sound so curt.

"Listen, I need to hang up now. I'll call you later." I wanted this conversation over and done with.

"Well, Robert and I will be out tomorrow afternoon." She hesitated. "Ah, better yet, we'll meet you at The Cheesecake Factory in Allen at one-thirty."

Why am I not surprised?

"Sure. I'll see you there."

"Oh, and Sage, bring this Garrett fellow with you. I want to meet him."

I glanced out the window and saw we had just passed Garrett's house. Why, hadn't I waited to call

150

Gabby until after I'd arrived home? Garrett didn't want to be pulled into our family get-together any more than I did, particularly since it could be heated. Then again, Garrett might be the stabilizing factor to keep Gabby and me from having words.

I can't do that to him

"I don't think he'll be able to make it."

"He's there with you now, isn't he?" Gabby's frustration level was rising, her voice pushy, demanding.

"Yes."

"Ask him. Tell him I want to meet him. Better yet, hand him the phone. I'll ask."

"Hold on a moment."

I buried the phone in my lap, plainly exasperated. Why she chose this moment to go all motherly on me, I couldn't comprehend.

I turned to Garrett. "I'm sorry I dragged you into this family moment we seem to be having. But Gabby and Robert, that's my stepfather, would like you to come to lunch with me at one-thirty tomorrow at the Cheesecake Factory in Allen. She insisted I invite you. Their treat."

I took a breath. "Just say no. That'll put an end to the matter."

He glanced at me, his brow crinkled, before looking back at the road. "Do you want me to say *no?*"

I really didn't. "I'd love for you come, only if you want to. But don't feel pressured."

"I don't." He smiled, probably trying to reassure me. "Tell her, yes."

Still covering the receiver, my brow puckered, I asked, "Are you sure? She took what I said about you being my friend to mean more." My cheeks were on fire.

"Tell *Gabby* I'll be there."

Laughing, I said, "She'll have a fit if you call her Gabby. She prefers Gabriella. I know I shouldn't, but I call her Gabby to get her goat."

"Like I said, tell *Gabby* I'll be there." He smiled this time.

I put the phone to my ear. "Garrett said he'd come."

"Good."

"We'll see you tomorrow at one-thirty. Bye." I wasn't going to give her another chance to ask more questions. I disconnected the phone.

"Listen, Garrett," I paused wondering how to start my explanation.

He looked at me and then back at the road.

"I'm sorry I used you to keep my mother from coming out to the farm tonight. I'll be better prepared tomorrow to see her. I just couldn't handle her. Not tonight."

"Sage, you don't have to apologize. I don't feel used."

"Yeah, but Gabby has read more into what I said. She takes the meaning of friends with a man to a whole new level. Gabby is thinking boyfriend, as in romantically involved."

"I can deal with that. And I really don't mind."

"Well if you're insistent on coming with me tomorrow, expect to be grilled over your pedigree, how we met, what you do for a living, and just how serious you are about me."

He shrugged, a strange, quirky smile appeared. "I'm cool with that too."

"Cool? How can you be cool when I've dragged you into a hornets' nest?"

Garrett pulled into my drive and then parked by the back door. Instead of getting out, he undid his seatbelt, turning toward me, quite serious.

"Listen, I don't know your mother, but from what I've gathered by the conversation, you two don't get along.

"That's an understatement. Gabby and I don't see eye-to-eye on anything. My vocation, my choice of living out in the sticks, as she puts it, taking care of Grams. Forget it. I'm too tired to go into it tonight."

"Don't sweat lunch tomorrow. It'll be fine." He grinned. "I'm a big boy. When I was young, I learned to watch out for the cow patties and step around them. I can take care of myself." His look turned from humor to dead serious. "But Sage, I won't sit around and allow Gabby to harass you if that's what she intends to do."

I picked at my nail, feeling awful having dragged Garrett into what I figured would be round one of endless rounds with Gabby trying to force my hand to her bidding.

That's just not happening!

"She can be ruthless, at times, wanting her own way."

Garrett looked ready for battle. "She hasn't met me. When it concerns those I love, no one's going to push them around."

He glanced down. "I know this may not be the time, with your Grams' passing and all, however, I need to make my intentions clear. I want you and me ... us to be more than friends. You may not believe this now, but I hope to prove to you over time that I'm falling in love with you."

His touch sent my emotions reeling and bouncing all over the place. I knew how I felt about

Garrett, which, if it wasn't love, was so close I couldn't tell the difference.

"I would like to see if what I … we feel, because I believe you sense it too, is the stuff marriage is made of. If you'll allow me, I want to be here for you. Hold you when you cry. And if I could, I'd brush away all the pain you are feeling at this moment." Swallowing, he looked deep into my eyes.

"Sage, I've never felt this way about another woman." He looked down at our hands, then back up at me. "Just looking at you, snatches my breath away. Since we've met, I've tried to keep my distance, but I can't." He chuckled. "I was miserable all week long without seeing you. That's the main reason why I showed up at the market this morning and this afternoon. I couldn't wait any longer. I had to see you — be near you."

He stared at me, his heart in his gaze.

I didn't know what to say. My eyes filled with tears. To think that a man like Garrett would love me was beyond imagination. And though I was still hurting from Grams' passing, wondering what I would do now that she was gone, I felt at peace with Garrett's words.

He turned to look out the front window. "I'm sorry. I've spoken too soon. I should have waited. This wasn't the time." He moved to open his door.

I touched his arm, stopping him.

"You may not know this, but Grams liked you, which said a lot." I wiped the tears from my eyes.

"Really?"

"Yes, really."

He grinned. "The feeling was mutual. Every time I stopped by with one pretense or another to see you, Grams always welcomed me with her sweet smile, and then she'd try to feed me." He smiled. "And her cooking was so good."

"I know. When you came knocking on the door the first time, bringing my hat home, Grams saw it as a perfect opportunity to play matchmaker." I chuckled. "I can still see her now, her cunning smile with that playful twinkle in her eyes."

I shifted in the seat. Memories of Grams were so sweet. "You should feel privileged. You're the only single young man Grams ever invited to dinner." I raised my brows. "Others came calling, but she never liked them enough to invite them. But you, she took an instant liking to."

"That means a whole lot to me. Thanks. I just wished I could have gotten to know her better."

He lifted my chin. "Since I know I have her blessing, I'm not going anywhere. I'm sticking around until I have you convinced I'm here for the long haul."

"I don't think you'll have to do much convincing." I couldn't believe I was being so bold.

"Good." He leaned toward me, his eyes shining with anticipation. "May I."

I knew he was asking permission to kiss me, which was sweet and a little old-fashioned, but I liked it. I nodded, the blood pulsing through my veins.

His soft butterfly kiss was over too soon. Yet, it was perfect.

"Sage, I meant what I said. I'm falling in love with you. However, I'll wait. You need time to grieve for Grams. When you're ready, regardless how long it takes, I'll be here."

"Oh, Garrett." My heart was too full to express my gratitude.

"I'll help with whatever you need. And when your heart is ready, my plan is to claim you as mine."

Garrett wiped the tears from under my eyes with his thumbs, and then ever so gently kissed me again.

Pulling back, he opened the truck door.

"There are chores I need to get done, and you have some business to attend to." He hopped down out of the truck, shutting the door, causing the quiet to close in on me.

Oh, Grams, why couldn't you have held on a little longer. I need you. And I so want you to know about Garrett. You would have been happy for me.

The promise of rain hung in the heavy black clouds, obscuring the sunset. My loss was magnified as dusk settled down around me.

When Garrett opened my door and saw me, he wouldn't allow me to climb down from the truck. Instead, he lifted me out of the seat and held my head against his shoulder. For the longest, he held me while I wept, soothing me with his quiet strength. When my tears subsided, he allowed me to stand, but held me in the circle of his arms.

Sammy nudged my leg and whined. He knew something wasn't right. Maybe he knew Grams had died.

Pulling back, I looked Garrett in the face. "I'm sorry. I'm …" I couldn't finish.

"Never be sorry for your grief. It's natural." He looked deep into my eyes. "Will you be all right while I do the chores?"

"You don't have to do them. I—"

He placed his finger to my lips to quiet my protest. "I do, and I will."

I slowly released my breath. "Yes, I'll be fine."

"Good. When I'm through, I'll take you to get a bite to eat."

"What if I treat you to leftover stew?"

"That's even better." He kissed me on the forehead, then released me.

I stood watching as he walked off toward the barn. Before he stepped inside, he turned and waved. Smiling, I waved back.

I felt blessed. Garrett in my life at this particular time was a Godsend. God knew I would need someone and He sent Garrett. And for now I would lean on him. But later ...

My heart checked me. *I will always need Garrett.*

Chapter 15

Garrett

"I won't be able to make Sunday dinner tomorrow."

I hoped Mom wouldn't ask why, but figured she would. Especially since both of my parents didn't take to the idea of me being interested in *the Anderson girl* as they called her.

"Oh. Why's that?" Mom sounded mildly curious.

"I'm going to lunch with a friend." I stepped into the chicken pen to put seed into the feeder. The chickens squawked like they were being abused.

"Is that chickens I hear? Did you buy some?"

Mom's hearing was as good as ever.

"Yes, it's chickens. And no, I haven't bought any. I'm helping a friend right now by feeding the chickens."

"Who's the friend?" I could hear her suspicion.

160

Might as well get it over and done with. I poured the feed, causing another outburst of squawking. "Sage Anderson."

"Sage? Am I to assume she's the one you're having dinner with tomorrow?"

I dusted off my hands, closed the chicken coop door, and then headed for Sage's old beat up truck. It needed to be unpacked, and I'd see what was salvageable from her leftover produce, if anything.

"Yes."

"If your father knew, he'd wouldn't be happy. But for now, I won't tell him."

Lifting the box that held a few jars of honey and canned goods, I headed for the barn, since it was the only building besides the house, it had to be the logical choice for storage.

"Listen, you can tell Dad for me, Sage is nothing like her mother. She's good, kind, and decent. And she just lost her grandmother."

"What do you mean, *lost her grandmother*?"

"Just that. Her grandmother passed away this afternoon."

I took a breath to calm my frustration for having to explain the situation. After setting the box on the table, I stood for a few moments, allowing my eyes to adjust to the dimly lit barn.

"Oh, the poor girl."

161

"You can say that again. Her grandmother was her world. It's hit her hard. That's why I'm here doing her farm chores while she contacts people, making arrangements for a funeral."

I opened a cupboard. Preserves and honey jars were lined up on the shelves with plenty of space for the few jars left in the box.

"Good. I'm glad you're there to help, Garrett. She'll need your friendship." She paused. "Is her mother there?"

"No. Sage is on her own."

"What a shame. She shouldn't have left the poor girl to do everything by herself."

I didn't remark, knowing I'd say more than needed to be said on the subject of Sage's mother, or lack thereof.

Instead, I took a look around wondering how Sage and her grandmother had made it on their own for the last few years. Everything was neat and tidy, but everything was in dire need of attention and repair.

The paint was non-existent or peeling. Some of the old wood siding had issues. Even the roof looked like it wouldn't keep out a good storm. This farm needed serious help.

"From what I heard from Sage's conversation with her mother on the ride home, they don't exactly get along."

My mother's snort said it all. "I can believe that. All I can say for Gabby is, if she's anything, she's predictable. Sage is to be pitied." Again she made a disgusted sound. "But people do change. So I won't say more. All I ask is you be careful. Make sure Sage isn't anything like her mother before you get too involved with the girl."

"Mom, I'm a grown man. I can look out for myself and make intelligent decisions when it comes to my life. I don't need advice or help."

"I know you can. However, that doesn't stop me from worrying about you."

"Hey, listen. I need to let you go. It's been a while since I've checked on Sage."

"All right. Let her know that she's in our prayers. And if there's anything I can do, call."

"I will. Love you. Bye."

Mom thinking Sage could be anything like her mother was preposterous. The fact that Sage took care of her grandmother proved she was different.

Sage was sweet, considerate, and had a fiery disposition, which would make life interesting. I smiled and continued unloading the few boxes left in the backend of Sage's truck before heading up to the house.

I knocked on the back door.

Sage didn't answer.

Thinking she might not have heard me, I opened the door. "Sage, it's me, Garrett."

Still no answer.

Worry gripped my gut. Where was she that she couldn't hear me?

Rushing through the kitchen, into the living room, I found her curled up on the couch, under an afghan sound asleep. She had a grip on the cover like a child would their old raggedy blanky, one they could never part from.

In a quandary whether to wake her or allow her to sleep, I decided she needed the rest.

I sat down in one of the old, worn overstuffed chairs watching her.

Sage looked so peaceful and beautiful, even with tear swollen eyes. It was a challenge not to touch the few strands of hair that curled around her face. But I resisted.

Living in this big old farmhouse by herself was going be lonely. I hoped her mother wouldn't pressure her into moving back to Dallas. Not when we were just beginning to learn about our love for one another. I wanted Sage here, close to me so I could take care of her … if she'd let me.

Sage stretched like a lazy cat waking from a nap, and then sat up and stretched some more. I knew the moment she saw me. A rosy tint appeared on her cheeks. Her beautiful green eyes sparkled, which I hoped meant she was glad to see me.

"You're done?"

Grinning, I said, "Yes, sleepyhead. I'm glad you took a catnap. You needed it. Did you get everything done?"

I could have kicked myself for reminding her of her responsibilities and also Grams.

Her smile faded as she nodded. "How about you?"

"The only thing I didn't do was look at your cattle."

"I'm sorry I fell asleep." She stood, folding the afghan in half before throwing it over the back of the sofa. "Thank you so much for your help, Garrett. I'm sure you've got stuff you need to do. I'll—"

"The only stuff I have to do is take care of you and see that you're properly fed."

"Oh." She looked on the verge of crying again.

"You want to put on your boots and go with me to check the cattle?"

She brightened. "Sure. They're in the mudroom."

I followed her to the door and waited for her to slip her small feet into her boots.

She picked up her keys.

I took them from her hands.

"Unless these lock the back door, you can leave them here. I'm driving."

An old spark of fire showed up in her green eyes making the brown streaks look vibrant and alive.

I hoped she'd never get mad enough to tell me to leave because I'd try my hardest to convince her to let me stay.

"They lock the house."

I smiled, tweaking her nose before handing the keys back.

When I stopped the truck at the entrance to the back pasture, Sage hopped out before I could. She opened the gate, swinging it back, then grinned as she bowed and made a grand gesture with her hat for me to drive through.

This playful side of Sage, even in her grief, showed her strong character in the face of horrific circumstances.

For me, love was a hard word to describe. But looking at Sage, I knew I had found love and so much more in this small package of a woman. Now, if I could just convince her of the same, life would be sweet.

Chapter 16

Sage

"Are you going to be okay?"

Concern was in his gaze, then the look turned incredulous.

"Tell me, you do have something more than a broom for protection." He stood on the back porch, ready to leave.

A gurgle of laughter erupted. "Yes, I do. I have a shotgun, fully loaded by my nightstand."

"Good. Otherwise, I was going to go home and bring back a gun."

I walked Garrett to his truck.

He put his arms around my waist and drew me up close. "I hate to leave you here alone."

"I'll be fine." I rolled my eyes. "I have my cell phone with me always, my shotgun by the bed, and

Sammy always barks if anyone strange drives on the property. So stop worrying."

I knew I really wouldn't be fine without Grams in the house, and now without Garrett. His words reinforced my situation and my aloneness.

He leaned in and gave me a light kiss. "You have my number if you need me."

I nodded, when what I really wanted to say ... *I need you now. Don't leave.* But I knew I wasn't being practical. Maybe one day, though.

"I'll see you tomorrow. Now go inside and lock the door."

"You do know I'm a big girl. I can take care of myself." I gave him a sassy look.

"Yes, but it would make me feel easier knowing you're inside behind locked doors when I leave."

His concern for my safety made me feel loved and secure. "All right. See you tomorrow."

"Wait. First I need to do this again." He leaned in and gave me a kiss that nearly curled the toes of my boots. After that kiss, I wasn't sure if I would be able to walk straight, let alone go inside and lock the door.

Garrett waited until I shut the backdoor before he started his engine.

I leaned against the door, reliving our kiss until I couldn't hear the sound of his truck anymore. The reality of being alone hit me square in the face, squeezing my heart until I thought it would burst.

I slid down the door into a heap, feeling so desolate and abandoned.

All my sweat, hard work, and barely getting by, had paid off. I'd provided Grams' her last wish—to live and eventually die in her own home. I just didn't know her leaving would be so soon.

I trudged up the stairs into my room to draw my bath, adding Grams' favorite rose fragrance to the tub. I climbed in, sliding down in the warm water, my tears mingling with the rose scented suds. I cried until the water was cold and my tears were spent.

When I finally crawled into bed, I couldn't sleep.

There were no gentle snores coming from Grams' room.

The house moaned and groaned with the wind. Or was it for the loss of the gentle woman whose love knew no bounds? She loved me when no one else did.

I thought I couldn't cry more ... I did.

***

At 5:00 am, my alarm woke me from a disturbed night of sleep, filled with bizarre dreams and outlandish endings. I brushed them from my mind while I got dressed in my grubby jeans, ratty t-shirt, and bright pink socks. I pulled my hair back into a bushy ponytail.

I really didn't want to face the day ahead. It wasn't the chores that bothered me or another day without Grams, I knew she was in a better place. My angst was over lunch with my mother, and hoping she would be civil to Garrett.

After Garrett met my dysfunctional mother, he'd probably wash his hands of me. I prayed he wouldn't.

Heading down the stairs, the house was unusually quiet. Absent were the smells of coffee brewing on the stove, bacon frying in the skillet, and Grams' flaky biscuits filling the air.

The hollow feeling inside made my hunger evaporate. So much of my life was tied up in Grams. Now everything—my struggles, the farm, my work all seemed pointless.

A knock on the back door had my heart pumping. This early in the morning, someone had to be up to no good. I grabbed the broom and peeked out the backdoor window into the darkened sky. My porch light shined down on Garrett's head holding a white box in his hands.

I unlocked the door, then pushed it back smiling. "Hi. What are you doing here so early?"

"I came to help with the chores and I brought breakfast." He was grinning until he looked at the broom in my hand. His brow puckered tight. "I thought you said you had a shotgun for protection."

"I do." I smiled. "It's upstairs." I leaned the broom against the wall before heading to the kitchen.

"A lot of good it does you up there when you're down here."

I ignored him. "Breakfast, you say. Come in. I'll put on a pot of coffee." I was so happy to see Garrett I wanted to run into his arms. "Have a seat."

He set the box on the table and then opened the lid.

The air morphed into something sweet and salty, causing my stomach to rumble and my appetite to turn ravenous.

While I got the coffee started, Garrett set plates on the table.

"You not only know your way around a farm, you're domesticated too," I teased. "You're a handy guy to have around."

"Thanks, I'm glad you feel that way." He came over to where I was leaning against the sink, pulled me into the circle of his arms, and then looked down into my eyes. "Did you sleep well last night?"

"No." I had to be honest. "The house was too quiet. I'm used to hearing Grams. But it'll get better with time."

"It will." He drew me closer, my cheek resting on his chest.

I could hear the rapid beat of his heart. *Did I do that to him?* I smiled.

His spicy cologne mingled with the smell of coffee. In his arms, I had the sense all was right with the world, when it wasn't. Still, I willed myself to believe the lie for a little while.

He took a whiff of my hair. "You smell like roses." He pulled back, looking at me. "From this day on, I'll never be able to smell a rose bush without thinking of you." He kissed me on the forehead, then stepped back, dropping his arms to his side.

"Regardless how much I'd love to stand here and hold you, there's work to be done, and I'm starved."

This was one time I would have rather forgotten about what was waiting for me outside the back door. I wanted to be held, feel the magic of Garret's love in his arms.

You ninny, you've fallen head over boots in love with Garrett.

He must have sensed my mood.

"Come here, you." He pulled me back into his arms and tipped my head up. "I've been wanting to do this ever since I left this house last night." Dipping his head, he captured my lips, giving me a sweet kiss that sent my emotions reeling.

Pulling back, he looked down into my eyes. "You're beautiful, you know that."

I shook my head.

"Let me show you then." Again, he kissed me.

He filled my heart with so much love I wasn't sure I would be able to stand on my own two feet if he released me, so I gripped his arms for support.

"Now you know how I feel. And hopefully, that may hold me for a little while." He smiled, and then released me. "I'm hungry."

To cover my new found feelings of love, I looked into the box of goodies he had brought.

"Yum, these look delicious. Where did you find a place open this early?" I watched Garrett with renewed interest, with the revelation I loved him … seriously loved him.

"Paradise Bakery. The owner is a friend of mine. She made these especially for me."

"Oh." Like a balloon being popped by a pin, his words stung. My hopes sank faster than a ship. Was he involved with the woman? Maybe dating her?

He grinned, as though he knew what I was thinking. "We went to school together."

"Oh." More disappointment. Theirs was a longstanding relationship.

"She's sweet on my brother, Justin. But it seems he has no time for her. So I try to encourage her to hang in there. One day, he'll realize she might be perfect for him." Garrett winked at me.

"Oh." Though my vocabulary had been reduced to one syllable, my hopes soared like a kite catching a renewed burst of wind. I grabbed a cinnamon roll and took a huge bite so I wouldn't say anything stupid like … I love you.

Garrett laughed. "Now I know what jealousy looks like, at least on your face."

Gulping down the bite, I almost choked. "What do you mean? I wasn't jealous." I tried for innocent but failed miserably.

"Could have fooled me." He chuckled. "Come here." He pulled me toward him and then lifted my chin before leaning in close. "You have some icing right"—he licked it off the side of my mouth—"there."

A shiver worked its way up my spine, as my cheeks flamed. I touched the spot he'd licked and cleared my throat. "Ah-thanks."

"Don't mention it." He went back to eating as if licking icing off someone's face was an everyday occurrence.

It was anything but ordinary to me. And it was something a lover would do.

"Do I need to dress up for Gabby and Robert?"

"What?" My mind was trying to catch up, but doing a miserable job of it.

"This afternoon for lunch. Do I need to dress up, or should I wear my overalls with one strap dangling and stick a piece of straw in my mouth?"

Again my face heated. "You heard?" I wanted to crawl in a hole.

"It was kind of hard not to hear her when she wasn't exactly quiet with her depiction of me."

"I'm so sorry." I rolled my eyes. "That's Gabby. She doesn't care who she hurts, she speaks her mind. I believe you may be in for more of the same this afternoon." I watched him closely. "If you'd rather not, you don't have to go. I won't think any less of you if you back out now."

"Listen, I have no intention of backing out. I'm too curious."

I wrinkled my brow. "About what, Gabby?"

"Whether she'll see me as the country hick, or someone who is her daughter's equal."

I laughed, shaking my head. "Garrett you are more than my equal. However, to Gabby, I don't believe she would like anyone who owned his own farm and lived in the country, even if you were as rich as Midas. She has an aversion to anything less than white-collar professionals. Even though without people like us, there'd be no food for her to eat at her high-dollar restaurants."

"*Whew!* You unloaded a mouthful." He laughed. "You haven't scared me off, though. Now I'm going just to see if I can't win the old dragon over."

I chuckled. "She'll love knowing you referred to her as the old dragon."

He motioned to the roll I still held in my hands. "Don't worry about it. I've got this handled. Now eat up. We still have work to do."

"Dressy casual."

At first he looked confused, then he grinned. "Dressy casual it is." He forked the last bite into his mouth.

A little piece of icing got stuck above his lips. I wished I were brazen enough to lick it off like he did me earlier, but I wasn't. Still the thought caused my emotions to race off the charts.

Whether or not Gabby liked my choice in Garrett, it didn't matter. Because I did.

But as far as the farm was concerned, I knew Grams was the glue that kept this place and me together. I wouldn't be able to stay on the farm since Grams' house was mortgaged to the hilt to my stepfather's bank. And Gabby would make certain the bank foreclosed to get me back to Dallas.

Chapter 17

Garrett

Sage was too quiet on the ride into Allen. All of my remarks fell on deaf ears, or if she answered my questions, I received monosyllabic answers.

She nervously picked at her cuticle, fidgeted with the top she wore, which really looked good on her, and constantly glanced out her window, her mind elsewhere.

What kind of a tyrant was Gabby to have Sage so worked up over a lunch meeting?

"We're here."

"Huh?" She looked at me, and then out the front window, biting her lower lip. She looked at her watch. "We can go on in, but I don't think Gabby will be here yet."

"Which would you prefer?"

"Might as well go on in and get a table." Again she bit her lip.

I wanted to pull her into my arms and kiss her till she couldn't think of anything but me. I nixed that notion. Instead, I got out, and then went around to open her door to help her down.

When she got out of the truck and I didn't move out of her way, she looked up at me confused.

"What's going on?" I stared down into her beautiful face.

"Nothing." She shook her head and avoided looking at me.

"Please, tell me it's not me."

"Garrett, it's not you. You've been so helpful and sweet about everything. My problem is Gabby. I never know what to expect from her. Either she's on the attack or overly friendly."

"Sage, Gabby can't hurt you unless you allow her to, and as long as I'm here, I won't let her. Just remember, I'm on your side."

"I know." She bit her bottom lip again, tears forming in her eyes.

Touching her lip, I gained her attention. "You've got guts, Sage Anderson. Show her she can't steamroll right over you. Make her see the grown, beautiful woman you have become. Show her that fearless person who faced down a man nearly twice her size, without flinching."

I chuckled when my mind conjured up the hellcat covered in lettuce leaves. "You got me to pay almost triple for a bunch of damaged lettuce."

"I tried to pay you back." She looked indignant.

"You did. But this isn't about lettuce or money." I waved her off. "What you don't know and I didn't realize, our first accidental meeting was the day I fell in love with you."

"You really love me?" The childlike sound tore at my heart.

"If thinking of you constantly, wanting to hold you in my arms and never let you go, needing to hear your voice is love, then yes, I love you." I smiled, pulling her into my arms. "I don't know how it happened so fast, but it did. And now, I can't seem to get enough of you."

"Garrett, are you sure?"

"Yes." I gave her a quick kiss before releasing her. "I think we better go in now, or I'm liable to embarrass you." I winked at her and watched her blush.

She wiped nervous fingers under her lashes. Standing on her tiptoes, she looked in the side view mirror on my truck to check her makeup, then looked back at me.

"Do I look okay?"

I tweaked her nose. "In my opinion, you always look gorgeous. Today, you look even more so."

Her smile and the sparkle in her eyes left me wanting to do more than lead her into the restaurant.

Inside, I told the young women we were expecting two more, gave her the name, and then asked for a booth in a corner as far away from other people as possible.

We were seated in a half round booth, tucked in a corner. Sage scooted in, but I stopped her from scooting too far from me. I wanted her near me, more as a collective front, if it came to that, but also because I preferred the feel of her next to me.

"Renee, dear, you look positively wretched."

Confused, I looked up in time to see the woman addressing Sage. She gave her the once over, at least as much as she could see, before her hard stare landed on me.

Grabbing Sage's cold hand, I moved it onto my lap, giving it a squeeze for reassurance, interlocking our fingers.

Gabby Stanford could only be described as an uppity, skinny woman, dressed in money, with a permanently arched brow. If she had red hair when she was younger, it was dyed to near black now. A few of her features, the high cheekbones and small turned up nose, Sage had inherited from her, but thankfully nothing more.

Robert was average and a man who seemed to stand in his wife's shadow.

"Hello, Gabby." The steel was back in Sage's voice. "You look the same as always."

I wanted to applaud Sage's grit, and say, *Hear! Hear!* But I smiled instead.

Sage looked past her mother to her stepfather. "Robert, nice to see you again."

The man nodded, "Sage, how are you doing?"

"I miss Grams, but I'm doing okay. Thanks for asking." She turned to me.

"Garrett, this is my mother, Gabriella, and my stepfather, Robert Stanford."

Releasing Sage's hand, I stood to shake hands.

"This is my friend, Garrett McCasland."

The intake hiss of breath and the narrow-eyed stare by Gabby wasn't missed. She knew my pedigree. I knew her history.

By the look on Sage's troubled face, she wasn't aware of her parent's jaded past.

"A pleasure to meet you. I believe you know my mother and father, Kayla and Gavin McCasland."

Gabby recovered nicely. "Yes." She gave a small laugh. "I used to date your father when I was in high school. How are your parents doing?"

"Very well, thanks." I shook Robert's hand. "Nice to meet you, sir."

"Same here, Garrett." The man studied me, evidently to see if I measured up to the country bumpkin image or if I was worth more.

Through with the pleasantries, Gabby slid into the booth, and Robert and I sat down.

"Have you ordered?" Gabby lifted her menu.

"No, just tea. We were waiting for you."

Everyone sat quietly while looking at the menus. The waiter came, took our orders, and left.

"What have you accomplished, Renee? And what do I need to do? Money, of course." She puckered her lips.

Again, I slipped Sage's hand in mine and squeezed gently.

"No, I don't need your money. All you need to do is show up at the funeral."

"Just where did the money come from for Mother's funeral? You have no money."

I could tell by the vibes, Sage was having a tough time with this conversation.

"Grams set aside some money. She paid in advance for her funeral and burial. So everything is done." Sage took a sip of water. "Pastor Sanders will officiate."

Gabby shook her head. "I would rather the minister from—"

"I'm afraid not. Grams wrote down specifics of what she wanted done for her funeral and also the minister who would officiate. I've already asked Pastor Sanders. It'll be at the church."

"That's not—"

"Gabriella, if that's what your mother wanted, what harm can there be in following her simple wishes?"

Robert nervously fiddled with the fork on the table while speaking to his wife more sternly than I would have thought him capable. The amazing thing, Gabby didn't object to his interference.

Robert cleared his throat. "Sage, whatever your grandmother wanted or if you want something more than she planned, make sure it's done. And please, if she didn't have adequate funds set aside, see to it and then send me the bill. I don't want you to worry about doing her funeral properly."

"Thanks, Robert. That's very kind of you. But Grams had sufficient funds to make her funeral lovely and simple as she requested." Sage smiled. "Grams didn't want any fanfare, just a few of her favorite songs, and her pastor to say a few words. And she'll be buried by Gramps which was purchased years ago."

"Good, then it's settled." Robert leaned back on the bench. "Since Garrett was invited, I assume you don't mind talking about your grandmother's business affairs in front of him."

Sage looked at me.

I gave her a slight nod to let her know I didn't mind being included.

"No. Speak freely."

"Good." Robert cleared his throat. "I believe, the sooner her affairs are settled, the better. Less complications arise."

The man surprised me. He had more steel in his backbone than I originally thought.

"I agree."

"Good. Gabriella and I have discussed the matter of the farm at length. Since the farm is upside down on the mortgage, and it was co-signed by me, it will be sold. What little profit, if any, will go to you for taking care of your grandmother for the last several years."

"I didn't take care of Grams. She took care of me. My part was minimal compared to hers. She wanted to die in the home where she was married. I worked the farm to make that happen."

I was beginning to understand more about Sage than I had before. Now I knew why she was so tenacious and willing to work so hard. No wonder she went ballistic the day we met, thinking she'd lost all the profit for the lettuce.

Robert waved his hand in dismissal. "We all know Adeline couldn't have stayed in her home until she passed away without you being there. She was failing and needed care, even if she didn't want to admit it."

Sage stiffened beside me.

"I will offer the farm at such a price that it will be sold quickly."

"I had hoped to continue to stay on and make the payments."

"I'm afraid that's not an option." Robert's ruthless nature finally show up. "The only reason we allowed you to work the farm until now was because of your grandmother. I floated the loan then. I won't any longer. The place will be sold."

"If only—"

"Don't be difficult, Renee." Gabby looked down her nose at Sage.

Her mother's sharp tone had me wanting to tell her to *back off*.

Gabby glanced at her nails. "I've already spoken to a realtor. They will be out later this week to appraise the house and property."

"The next thing on the list." Robert moved back his cuff to look at his watch. "What you will do since you no longer have the farm? The job I offered you a few months back is still available. It pays a decent salary to begin with, and an opportunity for advancement. You would be a natural at the job."

Sage's agitation transmitted to me. She ever so gently removed her hand from mine, and then place both hands in her lap.

The act puzzled me.

She glanced up at her stepfather. "Thank you for the offer. But I'll have to give it some thought."

"Don't wait too long. I may be the president of the bank, but that doesn't mean I can hold the position open indefinitely. We have several interviews scheduled."

"Renee, don't be stubborn. Without the farm, you'll have to find work. You know you can't find anything worthwhile in Primrose." Gabby turned her nose up, giving me a challenging look. "It's not like you have any grand offers in the making. Your future is in Dallas."

I had sat quiet long enough. "Gabby, Robert, I may be stepping in uninvited, but Sage ask me to come. And she does have a future in Primrose. It's with me."

"What? With you? A farmer? What can you offer except for more mud-grubbing, back-breaking work, that will turn Renee old and wrinkled before her time?"

Gabby's sneer made me want to crawl across the table and strangle the woman.

Sage stared at me as if I'd lost my mind.

"Call me a country hick, if you want." I thumbed my chest. "But this bumpkin holds two masters' degrees, a Doctor of Law degree, and owns several prosperous businesses. I also teach at the community college, and have so many offers for keynote speaker that I have to choose carefully which I'll take. And, as you so succinctly pointed out, I have a farm."

I turned to Sage, reached for her hand, looking straight into her beautiful green eyes.

"Sage, this may not be the place, but I feel it is the time. I love you with all my heart. Will you marry me?"

Tears rolled down her face, and she tucked her chin.

I froze.

Had I expected too much too soon? Sure it had only been a little over a month since we'd first met, but still I knew I needed her more than breath itself.

"You've upset her with your foolish talk." Gabby was angry over her scheme being thwarted. She had no concern for her daughter.

"*Sage.*" I prayed she would say yes, but was afraid she'd turn me down. "You name the date. We can marry as soon as you want, or whenever. It's your decision."

She looked at me as if to read my thoughts.

I wanted to plead with her, tell her I was sincere and meant what I said, but couldn't with her mother and Robert present.

Gabby looked stunned and ready to bite a nail in two.

Her stepfather studied me with curiosity.

"Yes."

Her answer was so light, I wasn't sure I heard her correctly.

"Yes? Did you say yes?" I was stunned.

She smiled. "Yes."

Without giving another thought that we were sitting in a crowded restaurant with her mother and stepfather looking on, I pulled her into my arms and sealed the deal with a kiss. I couldn't have been happier if I'd found a million bucks alongside the road.

The waiter came to the table with our food. A disturbing quiet settled around the table.

Gabby looked perturbed.

Robert looked at me as if I were a would-be bank robber.

I didn't care. I had what I wanted — Sage.

What concerned me most was Sage. She sat next to me unusually quiet.

Was she having second thoughts? I did spring it on her without giving her any hint of what I was about to do, even if she did say yes.

Like a flashlight flickering on and off, the thought that Sage had said yes to get her mother and stepfather off her back ate through my mind faster than a skill saw cutting through a piece of wood.

Whatever the reason she said yes, I would convince her it was for keeps.

Chapter 18

Sage

Gabby's stony stare spoke loud and clear. Her mother loathed Garrett's proposal.

And another thing, she didn't like any displays of public affection. Meaning, I'd get an earful later. But why didn't she like Garrett?

From the moment Garrett asked me to marry him, the meal became strained. I never thought the meal would be over so we could leave. Garrett and I had things to discuss.

For one, he didn't need to rescue me. I could stand on my own two feet when it came to Gabby and her schemes.

Outside and ready to leave, Gabby grabbed me for a hug, which I thought was strange. Rarely did she hug anyone, especially me. When my loser dad got her pregnant and I came along, she put all her blame on me for being stuck, as she put it, *in this one horse town.*

She got her mouth next to my ear. "I'll call you later tonight, and we'll discuss this."

I knew what *this* meant. She was going to tell me how foolhardy I was, and do her best to make me change my mind about Garrett.

She didn't know the proposal wasn't for real. For some reason, Garrett felt the need to use the ruse to get me off the hook with Robert and Gabby.

Once inside the truck, we angled our way out of the shopping center complex, I figured this was as good as any time to get it said and done.

"You didn't need to rescue me. I'm a grown woman, Garrett. Gabby can't make me do anything I don't want to do. So why the proposal?"

I studied him for any sign of remorse or a flicker of regret.

He grinned. "Because I love you and want to marry you. Why else?" His brow wrinkled. "I believe that's the normal reason to propose. Or did I miss something?"

I dismissed his answer with a wave of my hand.

"You know what I mean. There hasn't been a whole lot of normalcy about our relationship, let alone, a reason to get married. You're not saving me from Gabby. She hasn't run my life for some time now. I can do perfectly fine on my own."

"You can't think I did all that back there for your mother, do you?"

His words and puzzled look gave me hope.

"Well, I ..."

"Hold that thought." Garrett made a few turns before parking again. He undid his seatbelt and then turned toward me undoing my belt before taking hold of my hands.

"I love you, Sage. Some people may not believe I could love you this soon, but I do." His gorgeous blue eyes sparkled. "I want to move mountains for you. Love you all your days. Hold you when you're hurting, like now. Laugh with you when you're happy, even cry with you, which, if I have my way, will be seldom."

He smiled, squeezing my hands. "The only question I have for you ... do you love me?"

"Garrett, I-ah, how can I know what I feel for you is love, and not some fantasy. We barely know each other. What if this is just emotions run amuck?"

"Never going to happen." He lifted my hands and kissed the backs of them while looking into my eyes.

The touch of his lips caused my stomach to tighten, sending waves of emotion through my body.

194

His eyes held me captive. Even rational thought deserted me. How could a man like Garrett love me? My heart said I loved him, but was it too soon?

"Sage, marriages have lasted a lifetime and yet been built on a lot less than we have right now."

"I know. But what if—"

"Where's that girl with all the fire? The one who isn't afraid to believe? *Huh?*"

His intense gaze burned a path to my heart.

"Where's that tenacious woman who'd come after a full grown man over a basket of lettuce. Where is she?" He raised his brow. "That's the girl I fell in love with. That's the woman I want to marry." He smiled. "I love you, Sage Renee Anderson. Without you, I'm nothing."

"In my heart, I believe I love you, but …" I hesitated to ask my next question for fear I would anger Garrett. "Will you give me time?"

"Time?"

"Yes. Right now, my mind is on overload. If I have to process one more thing, I'm afraid it will burst. But I don't want to lose you."

"Babe, you'll never lose me." Again he kissed the back of my hands. "I'll give you time, only if you'll do one thing for me."

"I'll try."

"Wear my ring."

I looked at his fingers, plainly puzzled.

He shook his head. "No. I want to buy an engagement ring for you to wear."

My heart stopped. It started pumping like I'd just run up a hill.

"No stipulations apply, except for one."

Figuring it was too good to be true, I waited.

"If you ever decide you don't want to marry me, just give me the ring back. There'll be no questions asked. You'll break my heart, and I'll have a lot of regrets, no questions."

"Wouldn't you rather wait until I can say yes when I truly know my mind?"

"I know for sure I love you, and I believe you love me. However, there's too much going on right now for you to process how you feel." He grinned. "And, no, I'd rather you wear my ring. That way you'll know I mean business."

"Ah, Sage." He touched my cheek. "You'll soon learn, I love you beyond reason." His grin was filled with mischief. "And when you're wearing my ring, JD, or any other man, won't get any ideas you're free."

"JD? JD Robertson?" Mystified, I said, "What does JD have to do with us?"

He scowled. "You've got to be kidding. Haven't you noticed how he looks at you, with those big ol' puppy dog eyes."

"Puppy-dog eyes?" I started laughing. "You've got to be kidding."

"I'm not."

"JD's just being friendly."

"His kind of friendly, I can do without." Garrett was dead serious.

Again I laughed, quite baffled by his reaction to JD.

"Listen, as far as JD goes, you can rest easy. He is one man I have no interest in whatsoever."

"Good." He looked kind of sheepish while he played with my fingers. "I've learned something about myself since I've met you that I didn't know before."

"What's that?"

"Where you and other men are concerned, I find I'm extremely jealous." He grinned. "And I've never felt jealous before."

"Don't be." I glanced down at my hands afraid to say the words. "I love you, if what I feel deep inside me is love. But ..."

"Never have liked buts." He lifted my chin and stared into my eyes. "Let's leave it at *I love you*, okay?"

I nodded, pulling my bottom lip through my teeth. He touched my lips.

"Sage, I won't pressure you for more. When you're ready, tell me, and we'll set the date. I'm perfectly fine knowing you love me and you want to be sure before taking the next step. When that day comes, I'll do handsprings. Until then ..." He leaned in and kissed me.

He winked. "What do you say we go pick out a ring?"

"Oh, I don't know."

"Hey, listen, you don't want to trust my tastes. My sister, Issy, says I have no sense of style when it comes to picking out things for women. She always goes with me when I'm buying a present for mom. So please, don't make me buy it on my own."

"Speaking of family ..." I hesitated, trying to formulate my thoughts. "What will your family say about us?" This was a real issue with me.

"Mom will be tickled pink one of us is finally tying the knot. Issy will be over the top. She's been trying to marry me off for the last six months to any number of her girlfriends until I hinted about you." He laughed. "She was going to come over and meet you until I put a stop to it. I didn't want her pestering you until I was sure you felt the same about me."

He opened the door, and then came around to help me down. Nodding at the store, he grinned. "This place should have plenty of choices. But if you don't find what you like, I don't want you to settle. We'll go somewhere else and look."

My heart beat triple time, knowing I was about to become officially engaged to this remarkable guy. It was too good to be true.

Wait! What about that old adage ... If it seems too good to be true, it probably is.

Lord, please, don't allow Garrett to wake up tomorrow and change his mind. If he did, it would destroy me.

Chapter 19

Garrett

By the time we walked out of the jewelry store, Sage had picked out an oval cut diamond with small diamonds trailing off each side.

When I told the clerk to put the ring in a box and bag it, Sage tried to hide her disappointment, but I noticed.

I couldn't wait until we were alone so I could propose properly.

"You mentioned your mother and Issy would be happy about our engagement. What about your father and brothers? What will they think?"

Taking the off ramp, I used the time to maneuver the curve and merge into traffic to think of how best to answer.

"You know men." I shrugged.

"That's just it. I have little knowledge of men, except for all of Gabby's boyfriends, when I was younger. They weren't much of an example. And then living with Grams, we were two single women with little male interaction. So you'll have to clue me in about your father and brothers." She stared at me, her head tilted to the side.

"They'll say congrats, then go back to whatever they were doing." At least for now, I thought it best not to tell her my father had warned me to stay away from that Anderson woman. Dad didn't think much of Gabby for her trying to break mom and him apart. And my brothers seemed none too happy.

Sage held the satin sack with the ring inside and fiddled with the ribbons. Her nervous actions clued me in on her thoughts.

"Listen my family will love you."

Her brow wrinkled, while her fingers continued to fidget.

I patted her nervous hands. "Babe, they will love you like I do." Grinning, I added, "Well, maybe not the way that I love you, but they'll love you, just wait and see."

"Have you told them about us?"

"They know I'm dating you, but ..." Her nervous gurgle of laughter stopped me.

"What's so funny?" I took a quick glance at her.

"Dating? You could hardly call going out two times and doing farm chores together as dating. What will they say when they find out we've only known each other a little over a month?"

"You're really worked up about them, aren't you?"

"Yes. They're important to you. They'll be important to me when we get married."

Realizing she hadn't hedged around our marriage, I smiled.

"Garrett, this isn't funny. This is a serious matter."

"I'm sorry. But I smiled because you said *when* we get married, not *if*."

"Well ..." Her cheeks turned red, a small grin appeared. "Back to your family. I want them to at least like me a little."

I turned into Sage's drive. "Hang onto that thought." I pulled up and parked. "Do you think we could go inside for this discussion?"

"Okay. Here." She held out the bag with the ring inside. "Not sure what you want to do with this."

Put it on your finger, love.

Without answering, I just got out of the truck and then went around to help her out.

Sage turned up the thermostat and then led me into the living room. When she started to sit down, I stopped her.

"I want to do this right. I botched it up at the restaurant."

She smiled, then went all nervous on me again.

Opening the silk sack, I pulled the box out of the bag feeling more nervous now than I had in front of Gabby and Robert.

"Sage, if someone had told me a few months ago that I would fall for one beautiful, spitfire of a redhead, I would have laughed in their face. But that was before I met you, or actually, before I dumped lettuce all over you." I grinned, taking her left hand.

She released a nervous laugh. Her cold fingers felt so small in my palm, yet so right.

"I love you with all my heart, and will for the rest of my life and beyond. I want to hold you, love you, and show you we can make the world a better place together." He swallowed. "I can't think of anyone who would make a better mother for my children, nor a better wife to stand by my side and grow old together. And I can't, no, I don't want to imagine life without you. Sage Renee Anderson, will you marry me?"

Holding the ring suspended above her finger, ready to slip it on, I prayed she wasn't having second thoughts and refuse me.

Her smile was radiant, her eyes shiny with tears, she nodded.

"Yes, I'll marry you."

A weight of her answer lifted off my shoulders as I slipped the diamond over her last knuckle. I pulled her into my arms, kissing her like there was no tomorrow. In that moment, I knew no one else could ever fill her place in my heart.

I pulled back, still holding her in my arms.

"You've just made me the happiest man in the world. And if I kiss you like that again, we'll have to get married tonight. Because I can't wait to claim you in every possible way as my wife."

At first, she didn't look at me.

"What's up?" I lifted her chin with my finger.

"When will you tell your family?"

Her look of concern wasn't lost on me.

"We'll tell Mom and Dad this week. I'll invite them to dinner. How does that sound?"

"You want me there?"

Her dubious expression was almost laughable, but I held a straight face.

"Definitely. I want them to meet you. And of course, Mom will want you to come next week to Sunday dinner to meet the rest of the clan."

When she looked ready to run, I laughed. "I promise they won't eat you alive. They'll love you."

"I know." She rolled her eyes. "As much as you love me."

"How'd you guess?" I grinned. "I'll have to warn you though."

She looked concerned.

"Once Mom and Issy find out we're getting married, they'll be all eager, wanting to jump right in and help you plan the wedding."

Sage pulled backed away from me then sat down on the couch. "This is really too much for me. Maybe we should keep our engagement a secret for a while."

I slid down beside her, taking her hand in mine, trying to see her thoughts in her eyes.

"No. I don't want to be sneaking around. I want the world to know, or at least my family, I'm marrying the prettiest gal in the state of Texas. No, nix that. The whole universe, if there's life out there in space."

She breathed in heavily, her shoulders slumping.

"The next few days are going to be difficult. I still have a lot to do before Grams' funeral on Tuesday. And since I'm being evicted, I need to find a place to live, a job, and do quite a bit of packing."

Her brows crunched together. "It sure would take a load off my mind if you could tell your mom and dad before we meet them for dinner. That way, they won't be so surprised."

"If that's what you want."

"Yes. You can answer their questions about us so there won't be any surprises. That way ..." She shrugged, turning her palms up as if to say *I'm sorry.*

"All right. I'll tell them tonight. Will dinner Saturday night work for you?"

"Saturday should be fine." Tears glistening at the edge of her lashes. She glanced around the room, twisting the ring around her finger. "Oh, Garrett, perhaps our timing is all off. Maybe we should wait."

"Come here." I pulled her into my arms, resting her head on my chest. "Our timing is perfect. I'm here for you. I won't let you go through this alone. Whatever you need, I'll see that it's done."

I held her, allowing her to cry until she stopped and then pulled back.

"Listen, I'll be here to do the farm chores. That way, it'll free you up for all the other things you need to do."

"I can't let you do that. You've got your own farm to look after."

"You can, and you will. My farm only takes a quick look, a few adjustments, and I'm done. I'll leave you my schedule, that way you will know the days I'll be here in the mornings. In the evenings, when I'm through, I'll help you pack or tote."

"What did I do to deserve such a perfect man?" Her smile, though a little watery, was gorgeous.

"Oh, I don't know. God must have had a hand in it. He certainly knew you were everything I've ever wanted in a wife, and so much more. And one of these days, when you're good and ready, we'll get married."

I scratched my jaw. "I just hope you won't wait too long. If you do, I'm not sure I'll survive."

Chapter 20

Sage

Thankfully, Gabby called while Garrett was outside taking care of *my* chores.

After spouting off about my poor choice in a man, then not receiving any reaction from me, Gabby settled down, *some*. She made it perfectly clear she wasn't happy I was engaged to one of the high and mighty McCaslands, who could do no wrong.

"Give me one good reason why you're so averse to Garrett besides *he's a high and mighty McCasland*." I waited for Gabby's response.

"That's reason enough."

Her flippant answer puzzled me. "What's going on. What are you not telling me?"

"Forget about the McCaslands. I found an apartment in downtown Dallas where you can move in by the first, which will work out just right. Once you move from Hicksville, you'll see Garrett isn't right for you."

I wanted to morph into a little atom, go through the phone and give her a good shaking. "I hope you haven't put up a deposit because I'm not moving to Dallas."

"Why are you being so pigheaded about this? You have a good-paying job waiting for you, an apartment overlooking downtown, what more could you ask for?" Gabby huffed out. "Furthermore, Robert has been more than forbearing dealing with you. We can introduce you into the right circles where you will find any number of intelligent, good looking young men, with a six figure income, and who are far superior to Garrett McCasland."

"Gabby, listen to me. I don't want to say anything I'll regret. However, if you're as smart as I believe you to be, get your deposit back, tell Robert thank you, but no thanks, and don't line up any men for me. I'm not moving to Dallas."

I breathed in and counted from ten down, trying to cool my temper.

"You'll end up a poor farmer's wife, spent and old before your time. Is that what you want out of life? I had higher hopes for you."

"You lived your life as you pleased, leaving me behind with my grandparents while you went jetting around the country. Only when it was convenient, or your conscience was pricked did you find time for me. So I don't believe you have a right to tell me how to live, or even think you know what I want out of life."

I took a breath to calm my anger. "My plans are to find a job, an apartment, and then, as you put it, become a farmer's wife. You can like it or not. That's your choice."

"You don't know what you're getting into. After you've made a mess of your life and you finally wake up, don't come crawling to me to make it better."

She hung up in my ear. And though troubled by Gabby's outburst and my response, the silence was refreshing.

Praying for grace and forgiveness for my temper, I pocketed my phone. Thankfully, I didn't have to continue with a conversation that would go nowhere and get more enraged with time. Yet regrets rolled through me for what should have been and started eating at my gut.

By the time Garrett came in, I was hurting so bad I could barely choke back the tears.

He noticed, opened his arms, and I flew into them, needing the comfort and love he offered. My heart was breaking from the loss of Grams, a mother who didn't care, and the uncertainty of my precarious situation.

Garrett held me until I could cry no more. I felt a little better.

"Would you want to go into town and get a burger?"

"No, I'm not really hungry." I motioned around the living room. "And I have to begin sorting through this stuff."

"Is there anything I can help you do?" He glanced around the room.

"No. This is something I have to do on my own, at least for now." I smiled. "Later, I'll need your help. But for now, you go on. You've done enough already. And I'm sure you have plenty of work of your own."

"True. But I hate to leave you."

"Don't worry about me. I'll start on those shelves." I pointed behind me. "Maybe later warm up a can of soup. According to Robert, I have a little under a month to get this house packed and moved. Not to mention, find a job and an apartment."

"I'll let the word out that you're looking for both. My brother, the cop, usually knows what's what in Primrose. He may know of a job. Or Issy might know someone who's hiring."

"Thanks, I appreciate any help in finding both."

I walked Garrett to the door.

"Come here you." He pulled me into his arms again.

He leaned his head forward, then kissed me, giving me a buzz all the way to my toes. When he pulled back, I was breathless. I held onto him for support. It was so easy for Garrett to shake me to the very core by a simple look or kiss.

"I'll send you my schedule tonight. Mondays and Wednesdays I teach. But I'll be by late afternoon. So anything outside, don't you dare touch. Leave it for me." He tweaked my nose. "Do you hear me?"

I laughed. "You're standing next to me. I'm not deaf."

"Good. I'll see you around three. And tomorrow night, I'm taking you to dinner to celebrate our engagement." He gave me a no nonsense look. "I love you."

He gave me a peck.

"I love you too."

"Go on inside and lock the door."

When I closed and locked the door, Garrett began whistling and continued until his truck door shut cutting off the sound.

Again, I leaned my back against the door and listened to the sound of his truck driving away. A more desolate sound, I couldn't imagine. I stood there until only the lonely beating of my heart and the haunting quiet of the house could be heard.

Pushing away from the door, I wrapped my arms around my middle as I made my way into the living room. The repressive quiet and the fact Grams was no longer here hit me full force. Everywhere I looked, reminded me of her, crumbling my will not to cry.

On the couch, I wrapped Grams' afghan around me. The soft smell of roses drifted up from the cover. Bunching it in my hands, I held the wrap to my face and breathed in deeply. The solitary act pushed open my floodgates of grief, racking my body, as the tears fell.

I wanted so much to talk to Grams, tell her how much I loved her, missed her, needed her. I wanted her to know about Garrett and me.

Would she be happy?

I believed she would. There was so much I had to tell her, but she couldn't listen to me or give me advice any longer.

***

213

Wondering how Garrett's Monday morning class was going, I shoved a basket of cucumbers into the barn fridge, glad to be finished with my morning chores. I walked from the barn and noticed a police car parked in the front of the house.

My heart jumped in my throat. The toast and coffee of earlier began to swim in my stomach, threatening to come up.

Garrett? Did something happen to him?

Don't be so foolish.

The police wouldn't know I was engaged to Garrett. If something happened to him, I'd be the last to know.

Dressed in a navy uniform, a policeman came from the front of the house. He wore dark sunglasses, no hat, with a gun strapped to his side. Seeing me, he headed straight in my direction. The closer he got, I could see his grim expression, which gave me chills and a strange foreboding something was wrong.

Maybe Gabby or Robert.

"May I help you?" I shielded the sun from my eyes to get a better look at him.

"Are you Sage Anderson?"

Again, the horrible feeling he was here to tell me something that would change my world, gripped my stomach. "Yes. What can I do for you?"

"I'm not here officially." The man was about Garrett's age but had an arrogance about him that I didn't like.

I wanted to scream, *get on with it*, but I held my tongue, figuring whatever he had to say couldn't affect me since he wasn't here formally.

As curious as all get out, I remained calm and smiled.

"I understand you just recently became engaged."

Now his words did affect me.

"Oh? Then I guess I'm to be congratulated." I stared at the man.

"Well, there might be some dispute as to whether it's to be congratulations or condolences."

Whoever this guy was, he had passed the point of being civil. His remark had tipped the milk bucket, so-to-speak. He had no call to be demeaning, not on my property. And not to me!

His offensiveness had my temper boiling.

If it had been any other time, I might have laughed it off. However, his remark came too soon on the hills of Grams' death and my argument with Gabby last night.

"If you're not here officially, I want you to leave." I smacked my dirty hands on my hips, knowing I must look like one of Charles Dickens' street urchins.

I could feel the guy's penetrating stare all the way to my stomach.

"What's your game? Are you after money? If you are, lady, you can forget it. You'll never get your grubby little fingers on one penny of McCasland money. It's all sewed up in trust. So back off from my brother and leave him alone."

His hate filled words nearly knocked me to the ground.

Garrett's brother. I recognized some of this man's features as Garrett's.

Which one was he, Matt? No Matt's the attorney. Nick? No, … Justin. That's the one.

"Justin, I would suggest you climb back in your squad car and leave my property before we both say things we'll regret."

He looked a little shocked that I knew his name, but not enough to back down.

First, my mother, and now Justin. Who else would object to our engagement?

He ripped his sunglasses off, holding them out, shaking them at me.

"You'll break it off with Garrett and leave him alone, or you'll regret it. Do you understand?"

Though I was anything but calm, I forced myself to relax.

"You, sir, have crossed the line. I have no intention of breaking anything off with Garrett. In fact, after my Grandmother's funeral and burial tomorrow, I will begin planning our wedding. I'll be sure you receive an invitation. And you can either attend or stay away. That's your choice."

I turned and headed for the back door, ready to cry my heart out.

Justin didn't know it, but I would never cause a rift between him and Garrett, regardless how much I loved Garrett. I would return the ring this afternoon and make some plausible excuse even if it rips my heart out. I'll never tell him about Justin or what he said.

A forceful grip pulled me to a stop, swinging me around to face a furious Justin.

Instead of showing fear, I closed the door on my panic and reinforced my courage. I could crumble in privacy after this lunatic was gone, but not now.

Jerking my arm free from his grasp, I ground out, "Don't. Touch. Me!"

For once, I wished I could kick the guy in the shin, give him an uppercut to the nose, and then knee him where it would hurt most. But this was Garrett's brother.

217

"I don't think you fully grasp the situation, lady. So let me try again."

Looking into Justin's eyes, I saw a man struggling to maintain his temper while unsure of what he was doing. He crossed his arms as a tic rotated up and down in his jaws. I figured it wouldn't take much for him to lose it. Would he hurt me?

No this was Garrett's brother. I couldn't believe him capable.

"You're messing with my family. That's something I won't allow."

He was wound tighter than a rubber band stretched to its limit, ready to snap.

"I can either play good cop and nod every time we pass on the road, or ... I can stop you for any number of minor infractions. Meaning ... lady, I will become your worst nightmare. You choose."

By sheer willpower, I kept my knees from buckling as a chill of fear ran up my spine. I prayed I wouldn't puke all over his clean uniform, but there was a fifty-fifty chance I would.

"Justin, I appreciate the warning. However, I have a warning for you." I pulled my cellphone from my pocket. "If you don't get in your car and drive off of my property, I'm calling the cops."

Raising my brow, I began to punch the number, hoping he would just leave.

He gripped my hand and the phone, squeezing tighter than was comfortable.

Panic came up in my throat, choking me.

Would he break my wrist to prove his point?

"It seems you can't be persuaded to break it off with Garrett."

I shook my head, unable to speak as I tried to pull my hand free of his grip.

He released me and then slipped on his shades.

"Have a good day. And ... you'd best drive very carefully. Otherwise you're liable to find yourself on the other side of the law and in jail."

Justin strolled, no, he practically swaggered back to his car. He gave me one final long, hard stare through his windshield before backing around, then heading out to the road.

Watching him until he was out of sight, I realized I was still reeling from my encounter. On shaky legs, I moved to the back porch. Holding on to the railing, I slid down onto the top step, burying my head in my hands. I willed my heart to stop the rampage in my chest, but it didn't.

I sat on the step until I realized I wasn't shaking any longer. The pain in my chest felt like a knife was being twisted in my heart.

Stubborn enough not to allow Justin's scare tactics cause me to break it off with Garrett, I twisted the ring on my finger. The diamond twinkled and shined brightly in the morning sun. In that moment, I knew, without a doubt, I had to give the ring back to Garrett.

What I had to do was best for all concerned, especially to ensure the McCasland family harmony. Garrett's close knit ties with his brothers made my solution to the problem simple, even if it was tearing me apart. I felt like I would die.

I loved him too much to allow him to marry me.

Standing, I dusted my rear off before going inside for a bath.

First thing, I needed to find a job … and not in Primrose. I couldn't live in fear of always running into Garrett. Seeing him happy with another woman would rip my heart out.

Chapter 21

Garrett

I hopped out of my truck. I was greeted by Sammy's soft *woof* as he came running over to me.

After looking forward to seeing Sage all day long, and then to find her truck gone, was disappointing.

I reached down to give Sammy a good pat on the head. "You don't know where your mistress is, do you, boy?"

The dog cocked his head to one side as if to say *and you're asking me?*

"I'll take that as a *no.*"

He barked, then pranced around my feet. I gave him a good scratching and rubdown then reached inside the truck for my hat.

The sound of Sage's truck coming down the drive was unmistakable and had me smiling. My heart beat like one of those double drum cadences as I watched her drive up and park. I could hardly wait to pull her out of the truck and into my arms to kiss her senseless.

The sun glinted off of her hair, turning it to a burnished red-gold. I waved, but Sage didn't respond.

Something wasn't right. I didn't know what, but I'd find out and do my best to make it right.

She turned off the engine and scrambled out of the truck, ignoring the backfire and the terrible racket the chickens were creating.

Laughing, I went over to see if there was anything I could help carry in.

Dressed in a green dress that hugged her tiny waist, heels, and her hair pulled back in one of those bun thingies, Sage looked like a woman who had stepped out of a business world magazine. I'd never seen this look before.

Though I liked it better with her hair down around her shoulders and back, I figured that was something I'd keep to myself.

I let loose a wolf whistle and an admiring once over. "Hey, beautiful, where have you been? You look amazing."

Though she would normally get all embarrassed at my compliment, she didn't this time.

"Thank you."

Her quiet response reinforced my notion, something was up.

"I was disappointed when I drove up and you weren't here. But I'm glad you're home now."

I pulled her into my arms. She felt a little stiff, but her kiss was warm and tasted so good.

Maybe it was my imagination.

I let her go.

She avoided looking me in the eyes. Instead, she turned to grab her purse off the front seat, then shut the door. Without a word, she headed straight for the house.

"Hey, what's wrong?"

"Nothing. What makes you think that?"

"The way you're acting?" My stomach tightened.

"I'm not acting any way." Her tone was terse as she kept walking.

"Wait a minute, please." I grabbed her arm to stop her, wanting her to look at me, talk to me, even yell at me if need be so I could find out what this was all about.

She looked down at my hand before jerking her arm free … her face livid.

"I'm sorry." I held up my hands trying to show her I meant no harm. "Did I say or do something I shouldn't have?"

My chest tightened as I racked my brain trying to figure what had her so upset. "Is it Gabby?"

"Right now, I'd like to get out of these clothes and shoes, then we can talk." She unlocked the backdoor.

"I'll start on the chores. Give you some time and then I'll be in."

Sage nodded, walked inside, and then shut the door, shutting me out.

Heading out to the barn, my cellphone rang. "This is Garrett."

"Garrett, I'm so glad I caught you." Mom's voice sounded tight and a little uneasy.

What's going on? First Sage and now Mom.

"What's up?"

"It's—well, your father can't make dinner Saturday night. He wants you to come for dinner tonight, instead, and-ah bring Sage with you. I've cooked plenty and it's your favorite. Pot roast."

"I'll call you back once I've talked with Sage."

"All right, thanks."

"I'll give you a call in about thirty minutes. Later." I hung up, the whole conversation turning over in my brain.

Dad never requested someone to come to dinner unless he wanted to talk with them. Meaning … something wasn't right and Dad meant to straighten it out.

I decided to do the immediate chores before going to the house to talk with Sage. By the time I completed them, it was well past the half hour to call mom back.

On the porch, I knocked on the backdoor and waited for Sage to answer.

The door opened and there stood Sage still in her clothes, no shoes, and her hair hanging around her shoulders, and … she'd been crying.

"Ah, babe, what's wrong?" I reached for her.

She shook her head, crossed her arms over her middle, but scooted back so I could enter.

Something inside me told me not to touch her, though I ached to do so, wanting to gather her in my arms and wipe the hurt away.

I followed her into the living room. She chose the old overstuffed chair sitting cross-legged, hunched over a pillow, pulling at the fringe.

I chose the couch, as close as I could be to where she sat.

"Am I to play fifty questions? Or are you going to tell me what this is all about?"

225

I watched her closely as she chewed her bottom lip, not looking at me.

"If you remember, I told you I didn't think this—you and me—would work." She motioned first at me and then at her.

"You haven't given us a chance. Don't throw away what we have together." I ran a hand through my hair. "I should have waited. For you to deal with your grandmother's death, and then me, it's too much." Glancing up at her I said, "I don't want to lose you, Sage."

"Garrett, you don't understand."

"I'm trying to. I love you, and because I do, I'll back off for the time being, if that's what you need. But don't shut the door on what we have together, please."

Chapter 22

Sage

Now that the time had come, I didn't think I had the nerve to follow through. Yet, what else could I do. I didn't want a rift between Garrett and his family. And that's what I'd cause by staying engaged to him.

Garrett stood, then began pacing the room.

"Please, Babe, don't do this. I know what we have is the real thing, if you'll just give us some time, you'll see it too. Give me a chance to show you how much I love you, and for you to see you love me."

I shook my head, holding back the tears. "We come from different worlds. It will never work." I bit my lip, looking down at the pillow in my hand, the tears blurring my vision. If I looked at Garrett, my resolve would melt.

"I found a job in Dallas today. And Gabby has a lead on an apartment, but I'm going to look around a little more."

"Why didn't you talk with me first? My brother, Matt, said if you can use a computer and do research, he had a job opening."

I twisted the ring and then began to slide it off my finger.

Garrett knelt in front of me, holding my hands, stopping me.

"Listen, please, don't make any rash decisions. Not now." He touched my chin, lifting my face to his. "Sage, I love you. Please give us a chance."

He lowered his face to mine, kissing me gently on the lips. This kiss was so different than all the others Garrett had given me. His heart and soul, even his fear, was rolled up in that one gentle kiss. He was begging me without words.

When he pulled back, still holding my hands, I knew I couldn't break it off with him. Not today, anyway. And not tomorrow. Maybe after Grams' funeral, maybe then I'd be strong enough to give him up.

"Please, keep the ring, wear it. Give me one week to prove our love is one that will last a lifetime. I need you. You need me. We're good together"

Breathing out heavily, my resistance disintegrated. I couldn't take any more heartbreak, and I loved him beyond reason.

"All right. But I'm not making any promises. After Grams' funeral we need to sit down and have a serious talk."

The tears I'd been forcing back took that moment to race down my cheeks, along with relief. I would have Garrett for another week, and then I'd give him back to his family. Regardless if giving Garrett up killed me, I wouldn't come between brothers. I loved him too much to do that to him.

Garrett dragged the pillow off my lap, pulled me to my feet before gathering me in his arms. He held me tight, trying to absorb my hurt, not saying a word.

Garrett didn't realize our love was doomed from the start. There was one obstacle too high to hurtle. His brother. Justin had the power to tear us apart, regardless how I boasted about inviting him to the wedding. I could never do that to the man I loved.

While I cried over our loss, Garrett rocked me back and forth until my tears subsided, but my heart never stopped hurting.

Again, he tilted my chin up, this time his kiss was hungry, like food to a dying man. I took all the love he had to give, and then shamefully, silently begged him for more.

When he finally released me, he smiled. "Sage Anderson, this week is going to be one incredible week. Tomorrow, we will say our goodbyes to Grams, and then in too many ways to count, I plan on showing you just how much I love you." He tweaked my nose.

His cellphone rang. He grimaced and rolled his eyes.

"I forgot. Mom wants us to come to dinner tonight. She cooked a pot roast with all the trimmings."

He must have seen my hesitancy.

"Listen, if you don't want to, I'll tell her no." He pulled out his phone to answer. "Hi Mom. I don't—"

"Tell her yes."

I don't know why I said the words. To face his family would be a cruelty of the worse sort. Cruel that I would know what I was missing out on. Cruel that he would have to face his family again when I finally gave back the ring.

"Hold on a second." He looked at me while holding his phone down by his side. "Are you sure? We can do this another time."

"I'm sure. Tell her we'll be there." I whispered, not wanting his mother to hear our conversation.

I stood listening to Garrett talk to his mother, I tried to figure out why I'd just committed myself to what would probably be a family dinner interrogation. Maybe this way, Garrett would see just how much his family wasn't in favor of our engagement, and then he'd let me gracefully walk away.

He pocketed his phone, looking at his watch. "Listen, I need to go home and change before we have dinner with the folks. Are you going to go like this, or do you want to change?"

"I'd rather change and do something with my hair. What time is dinner?"

"When we arrive." He smiled.

I pursed my lips, shaking my head.

"Six. Six-thirty."

"Then why don't you go home and dress, and then come back for me. That should give me enough time."

"That works." He shrugged and then pulled me into his arms again. "Are we good?"

"Yes. But we really need to sit down and discuss a few things after tomorrow."

"All right."

He gave me a quick peck. "I'll be back in about thirty minutes."

I walked him to the door.

"I love you." He gave me a hopeful look.

I smiled, not wanting to encourage him with my avowal of love, but I could see his disappointment.

***

By the time we arrived at Garrett's family homestead, my stomach was in knots. The place was intimidating, with its huge, white rock drive-through portico stretching out in front of the massive two-story, white-stoned house. The windows with shutters looked like dark imposing eyes watching. Still it was beautiful.

Garrett must have noticed my nervous tension. He pulled up in front of the house, parked, and then laid his hand over mine.

"Listen, Babe, if you'd rather not go inside, we can leave. Having dinner with my folks isn't a deal breaker. We can do it another time when you're ready. I'll make our regrets. And that will be the end of it."

"No. It's just ..." I licked my lips trying to articulate the words without giving away the real angst of the problem—Justin hated my guts. Maybe, his family did too.

Shaking my head, I said, "I'll be fine."

"I tell you what. If at any time you feel uncomfortable or want to go home for any reason, just tug on my sleeve, and it's a done deal. We're outta there." He raised his brow. "Okay?"

"All right. But first, tell me, why do you love me?"

A quirky smile appeared as he gazed at me lovingly and squeezed my hand. "Ah, now, that's hard to put into words, but I'll try my best.

"Why does the sun rise and set without fail? Why do the waves roll into shore and then go back out to sea? Why does the moon shine in the sky?"

"Darlin', it just does. And it's the same reason for me. I just do. I love you so much that at times it hurts."

The brilliance of love shining from his face had me transfixed.

"Like now, if I don't kiss you, you're gonna see a grown man cry." He leaned over the console toward me.

Like a magnet, I moved in his direction. I put as much of my love into the kiss as I could, knowing I would have to give him up.

He leaned back a little to stare at me. "Well, now, that certainly calls for more. But if I don't stop, we'll be in a heap of trouble."

A peck on the window had Garrett pulling back. "I swear. Issy has some of the worse timing." He rolled down the window. "What do you want, pest."

"Just wondering if you're going to come inside or sit out here necking all night."

Issy's gurgle of laughter sounded sweet but caused my cheeks to burn.

"Haven't made up my mind yet." He wiggled his brows at me.

I ground out, "Tell her we're coming in."

He winked at me. "We're on our way." He rolled up the window. "Remember, pull on my sleeve."

"Don't worry about me. I'm a big girl."

My door opened, startling me. I don't know what I expected, but Issy wasn't a young girl. She was probably my age or a year or two younger, if that. She was beautiful, with her cinnamon-colored hair and dark brown eyes fringed with the heaviest of lashes. I would have killed to have her lashes. And her smile was too much like Garrett's. I liked her instantly.

"Hi, I'm Isobel. And Garrett wasn't lying. You do have beautiful red hair." She looked across me. "Garrett, I like this one. She's a keeper."

"Enough, pest, before you run her off."

Garrett got out of the truck and then came around to where Issy and I stood, arms hooked together. I wasn't sure if she was afraid I'd bolt or she was just being friendly.

Letting my arm go, she grabbed my hand, pulling it up to see the ring. "I can tell you right now, Garrett didn't pick this out. He has awful taste, except where you're concerned."

"Unhand my woman," Garrett growled playfully while taking hold of me and then walking up to the front entrance.

"*Woo-hoo!* My, how the mighty has fallen." She grinned. "Let me be the first to welcome you to the McCasland family, where we love fierce. We love hard. And we love long. And it looks like Garrett is no exception. Though for a while I had my doubts." She linked her arm through mine again.

This time, I was flanked on both sides. Not sure if it was for moral support or just plain friendliness on Issy's part.

"Thank you." I didn't know how else to answer this young woman who had taken me by storm.

"Is everyone here?" Garrett squeezed my hand.

"We're waiting on Justin."

Justin's name struck terror to my heart, causing my foot to falter. Would he mention our meeting earlier in front of the others?

Garrett glanced down at me worried. "You okay?"

"I'm fine, just clumsy."

"Be careful." He laughed. "I hate to tell you, but I'm afraid you're in for a treat."

His sarcastic warning wasn't lost on me.

"Mom didn't tell me the others were coming." He stopped short of the door, giving his sister a meaningful look. "Issy, go on in. I want to speak to Sage for a moment."

She bit here lower lip, glancing at us as if she knew something was up. "All right." She squeezed my hand and smiled, apparently feeling my reticence.

"I'll wait for you in the foyer."

'Thanks." He nodded.

When the door shut, he pulled me into his arms. "Listen, if you're not up for this tonight, just say the word, and I'll take you home, right now. No questions asked."

I lovingly touched his cheek. "As long as you stay close, I'll be fine."

"Don't you worry about that. I'll be beside you all night long."

He took my hand, and lovingly kissed my palm.

A bushel load of sensations exploded in me, making my emotions go wild, until the thought of seeing Justin again brought me down to earth.

"I may want to leave early." I watched for his reaction to see if my request bothered him. It didn't.

"We'll leave whenever you say."

"Tomorrow is going to be very emotional and hectic for me." I swallowed, trying to squelch the sadness. "However, after the funeral and when everyone has left, you and I will sit down and have a long conversation."

"I'm fine with that."

"OK then, I'm ready to go in."

"All right, but first, I need this." He pulled me in for a tight hug and breathed in deeply. "You smell so good, and feel even better in my arms."

His words made me feel special and so loved. He kissed me lightly on the lips then smiled.

"Now I'm ready."

"I can just imagine what Issy's thinking." I giggled. "Necking in the car and now on the steps."

"My little sister does have a way with words." He winked.

Issy's words only embarrassed me. Justin was the one who was causing my nerves to bounce all over the place.

I wondered what he'd have to say or if he would even mention his impromptu visit this morning at the farm? I prayed he wouldn't. But eventually, his visit would have to be addressed. Hopefully, not tonight.

Chapter 23

Garrett

Something was radically brothering Sage. I could feel it in my bones.

I didn't believe for a second her tension was over the funeral tomorrow, or even meeting my family for the first time. Whatever had her as skittish as a newborn colt, I wanted to fix it, but I didn't figure she would allow me to.

Later, when we were alone and had our talk, would be the time to ask what was bugging her.

I ushered her into the living room. "Mom, Dad, this is Sage Anderson." I turned to Sage. "This is my mother, Kayla, and my father, Gavin."

Mom hugged Sage. "Welcome to our home. I'm so glad you could come."

Dad held out his hand, his gaze appraising Sage like he would any blooded stock he was thinking about purchasing. "Nice to meet you, and welcome."

"Thank you. You have a lovely home." Sage looked around the living room.

I could imagine what was going through her mind, especially, if she was comparing her home with the McCasland spread.

"I didn't know until yesterday that you both went to school with my mother, Gabriella Anderson Stanford."

"Yes, we-ah all three went to Primrose high together." Mom smiled, shaking her head. "My, that was back in the days."

The only tale-tail sign Dad wasn't happy with the discussion of Sage's mother, was the slight tightening of his jaw.

I motioned to my brothers. "Sage, this is Matthew, the lawyer in the family, and the oldest son. And this one is Nicholas, my baby brother. He raises blooded longhorns."

"You better watch who you're calling baby." Nick gave me a fake punch on the arm. "I may be the baby, but I have you by two inches and I can still put you on the ground in ten."

"Ignore him. He's a braggart." I smiled, knowing what Nick said was probably true. We hadn't tested it in a while.

I nodded at Issy. "And, of course, Isobel you've already met."

"Nice to meet all of you." Sage held onto my arm with a death-grip.

"My what a lovely ring." Mom had spied Sage's ring. She turned her gaze in my direction. "Do you have something you were going to tell us?"

I sensed more than felt Sage squirm next to me.

"Yes, I've asked Sage to marry me, and she said yes." I couldn't keep the happiness out of my voice. And it felt good to let everyone know Sage belonged to me, even if she was still on the fence about her decision.

"Congratulations. And welcome to our family." Mom hugged Sage again and then me. "Well, let me see the ring."

Sage held out her hand as Mom oohed and awed.

Dad clapped me on the back, smiling. "Congratulations, son. You've made a good choice." He gave Sage a hug. "Welcome to our family, Sage. If this guy ever gives you any trouble, you let me know and I'll straighten him out."

"Thanks, but I don't believe I'll have to take you up on your offer. Garrett's one of the good guys." Sage smiled up at me.

I felt like grabbing her up and kissing her in front of God and everyone, but I didn't want her embarrassed.

My brothers hugged Sage, telling her she didn't know what she was getting into by marrying me. And then they gave me some good-natured teasing about me being the first to turn in my single status badge, among other things.

I didn't mind their razzing because I had Sage, and she was worth anything I had to go through for her to become my wife.

"I hope you're hungry, Sage. I've cooked plenty." Mom smiled, and then motioned to all of us. "Dinner is on the table and getting cold." She led the way into the dining room. "Justin called and said he was running late, paperwork or something at the precinct."

I felt a slight tremble and tightening of Sage's hand. Bending close to her ear, I asked, "Are you okay, or do you want to leave."

She shook her head and kept walking. "I'm fine."

240

I pulled out the chair for Sage, assisting her, and then sat down beside her. "Mom, everything looks delicious."

"Thank you." Seeing everyone in their place, Mom nodded at Dad.

"Let's bow our heads." My father's voice rang out as he said the blessing.

When he was through, we all said "Amen."

"We were so sorry to hear about your grandmother's passing." Mom held out the plate filled with roast and carrots to begin passing it around the table.

"Thank you. It's an adjustment. I'm still not used to her not being around."

"And you won't, dear, for some time to come, as is natural."

"Garrett mentioned that you were looking for a job." Matt forked a piece of roast off the platter onto his plate.

"I believe I found one in Dallas this afternoon."

It bothered me that Sage was still thinking of moving to Dallas. There was still time to convince her otherwise.

"Oh?" Matt looked at her and then at me puzzled.

I shrugged.

"That'll be a long drive from here. It'll take you well over an hour one way." Issy looked at Sage as if she hadn't thought about that aspect.

"What will you do about the farm?" Dad was busy pouring gravy over his potatoes.

"The farm didn't belong to me, it belonged to Grams. I just made the payments. My stepfather, Ralph Sanford, is putting the farm on the market. I've been told I have a month to move out."

"That seems pretty severe."

"Gavin, I'm sure there's more to it than we know." Mom turned to Sage. "If you need any help packing, Issy and I would be more than happy to help."

"Thanks, but Grams had pretty well organized everything beforehand." Sage cleared her throat. "I think she had a premonition."

"Well, that'll make it a little easier on you. However, just call if you need help. And don't you go lifting heavy boxes. Garrett or one of my other sons can do the toting."

"Where will you move?" Issy asked the question, but everyone looked at Sage for the answer especially me.

"It depends." Sage spooned some green beans onto her plate and then passed them on. "If I take the job in Dallas, I'll probably get an apartment there.

But, for now, I haven't decided. I'll make my decision after Grams' funeral.

"Well, if that job doesn't pan out for you, just let me know."

"Thanks, Matt, I'll do that. And I appreciate the offer."

"Have y'all set a date yet?" I could tell, Mom's casual question wasn't so casual.

"Not yet." At least I could get Sage off the hook on this one. "We're holding off for a few weeks. Sage has too much on her plate right now to even think about a wedding date. But once we do, you'll be one of the first to know."

"Know what?"

Justin walked through the entry of the dining room smiling, heading to his chair, which Sage occupied.

He stopped, glaring at her. "What are you doing here?"

Chapter 24

Sage

Stunned silence hovered in the room.

Garrett jerked up, shoving back his chair, ready to defend me. The only thing that stopped him from going around the table and coming to blows with his brother was my hand on his arm and my soft-spoken plea. "Please, don't."

He looked down at me, his brow furrowed, then sat down, locking his hand with mine, as he looked at me with concern.

"Justin, what in the world has gotten into you. Where's your manners? That isn't how you to speak to our guest." Mrs. McCasland looked crossly at her son, while he attempted to stare me under the table.

"Explain yourself." Mr. McCasland's stern command drew Justin's attention.

"You've always said, the fruit doesn't fall far from the tree." Justin pointed his finger at me. "So why would you allow *her* to come into your home and sit at your table when you know what her mother did, … what the Andersons tried to do to the McCaslands?"

My breath stuck in my throat as his heated accusations swirled in my head.

What had the McCaslands done? Or, for that matter, my mother?

"Sage is my fiancée. And as such, you will treat her with respect, or we can step outside."

"Bring it on, bro."

Garrett's body went rigid and ready for attack.

"Garrett." I tried to convey, without saying the words, how I didn't want him and his brother at odds because of me.

"That's enough!"

Everyone looked at Mr. McCasland.

I bowed my head wishing I were anywhere but here, wondering how I could get out of this horrible situation.

"We will discuss this later, in private. Our dinner is getting cold. You can either sit down and eat with us or wait until we're done."

What did my family do to the McCaslands to garner such hatred from Justin?

Up until yesterday, I wasn't aware that Gabby knew the McCaslands, let alone went to school with them. Even with that recent knowledge in hand, I didn't have a clue as to why Justin was so upset.

As if that was the most important thing at the moment, everyone started eating while I quaked inside unable to lift my fork.

The tension, so thick in the room, snuffed out the lively exchange of earlier.

Scowling, Justin moved around the table to the vacant chair next to Issy.

I wanted to leave, but I also wanted to hear what Justin had to say about my family, and why his hatred had found its way to me. If I left now, I might never know. Worse yet, Garrett might also learn to hate me, and that would turn my already shaky world upside down.

"Do you want to leave?" Garrett's hushed question wasn't quiet enough. Everyone looked at me.

I shook my head and smiled. "No, I'm fine."

What I really wanted to do was run home and have a good cry. I picked up my fork and took a bite of the excellent food that tasted like dust in my mouth.

The general babble of dinner talk went around the table, yet I heard nothing. Fortunately, they didn't ask me any questions. After taking a couple more mouthfuls and then pushing the food around my plate, I decided I couldn't stomach another bite of Kayla's excellent food. I placed my flatware on the plate, wiped my mouth, and then sat back listening while avoiding any glances in Justin's direction.

"Kayla, you've outdone yourself. The meal was delicious." Mr. McCasland patted his stomach.

"Thank you." Kayla smiled at her husband's compliment. "Are we ready for dessert then?" She glanced around.

"Let's postpone dessert until after Justin and I have had our talk." Mr. McCasland stood. "Justin, Garrett, we'll talk in the library."

"I'd like to hear what he has to say since it involves me and my family." I was surprised I could get the words past my mouth. I shook like Jell-O inside.

"Are you sure?" Mr. McCasland looked uncertain.

"Yes, please."

"Do you want me to handle this for you?" Garrett's concern was almost my undoing.

"No."

His subdued smile was filled with anxiety.

We followed his father and Justin out of the room, leaving behind quite a bit of speculation.

Though Garrett held my hand, each step got heavier as I wondered what I'd learn about my family and their involvement with the McCaslands. Still, I had to know if Garrett and I were to have a ghost of a chance at love and a successful marriage.

"Please." Garrett's father motioned at the chairs and couch. He sat down in one of the wing backed chairs.

Garrett led me over to the couch and sat down next to me, still holding my hand. His love gave me the added strength I needed to face whatever Justin would expose.

"Sage, I'm sorry that you were dragged into this by my son, Justin, this evening."

Justin looked none too happy.

"However, Justin, being the third oldest of my children, has eyes that miss nothing, and a mind that retains just about everything he hears and sees, including when he eavesdrops on his parents' private conversations."

"So what does that have to do with Sage or her family?" Garrett's emotions were wound tight in defense of me.

"I'm getting to that, which makes me none too happy that Justin would bring up something that shouldn't have been brought up in the first place." Mr. McCasland cocked a brow.

"Mr. McCasland—"

"Please, call me Gavin." His smile was pleasant with a hint of regret.

"Gavin, I'm truly in the dark as far as my family's history is concerned. I hate to admit it, but the only family history I know about was gotten in the same manner as Justin—eavesdropping on conversations when no one thought I was around."

I took a breath, trying to gather my thoughts. "I also know my mother got pregnant with me and the man wouldn't marry her. Also, having me outside of marriage put a rift between my grandfather and Gabby. Other than that, what you have to say will be news to me. So please, enlighten me as to why Justin seems to hate my family and me enough to come to my farm and threaten me so I wouldn't marry Garrett."

"He did what?" Garrett looked at me then glared at Justin. "When was this? Today? This morning?"

Garrett might have been strung tight moments ago, but now he was ready to leap off the couch and lay into Justin here and now.

"I'm sorry I mentioned it." I glanced pleadingly at the men around me.

"Did you go out to Sage's this morning?" The blood vessels popped out in Garrett's neck as he stood with balled fists at his side.

I tugged on Garrett's hand.

He looked down at me. "Was your reticence this afternoon because Justin threatened you?"

"It doesn't matter."

"It matters to me."

"What if I did? I was protecting you from doing something stupid." Justin stood facing Garrett.

"Sit down, both of you!"

Gavin's harsh command got everyone's attention. He waited until both men stopped glaring at each other and then sat down.

"Again, Sage, I will apologize for my sons. It seems they are both a little hot tempered where you are concerned, each for much different reasons."

I knew Garrett's reason—love. But I was still puzzled as to Justin's.

"I'll make my tale as brief as possible so as not to belabor the facts." Gavin brushed a hand over his eyes. "Where to begin."

He took a deep breath then looked at me.

"All through our junior year in high school, Gabby and I dated. When she started looking at other boys and then dating them behind my back, I broke it off with her. At first, Gabby didn't seem to care so much, that is until a new girl moved into town, Kayla. I was smitten with her from the first day I laid eyes on her, and have been ever since." Gavin smiled at the memory, then seemed troubled.

"Gabby wasn't happy one wit about Kayla, so she did whatever she could to make Kayla miserable, and get me to go out with her again. She almost broke us apart."

"That was high school. Surely, that can't be what this is all about." I knew it had to be something worse than a petty high school break up.

Gavin took a deep breath. "No, I'm afraid it's much worse. When Gabby got pregnant with you, she told Kayla she was carrying my baby."

My gasp filled the room, as I searched Gavin's face for the truth.

"No, dear, I'm not your father, it was an older man. I had never slept with Gabby, to which she finally confessed the fact. Years later, when Kayla was expecting Isobel, Gabby came back to town and stayed with your grandmother. She tried once again to get her toy back." He hesitated as if he didn't want to continue. "Me."

Garrett squeezed my hand when he heard my intake of breath.

"She went too far when she told Kayla that she and I were having an affair when we weren't."

My stomach turned. What food I'd eaten was on the verge of coming up.

I chewed on my lower lip. How could I face Kayla knowing what my mother had done? Garrett and I could never get married now. I would be a constant reminder of what my mother had tried to do to this family.

What must Garrett think?

My humiliation knew no bounds. I didn't know what else to say as I attempted to pull my hand from his. He wouldn't allow me. Rather than make a scene, I stopped pulling. "I didn't know. I'm so sorry."

"Don't be." Kayla entered the room shaking her head. She shut the door behind her before moving to stand beside her husband. "That was over twenty-three years ago, dear. I've forgiven Gabby." She glanced lovingly at Justin. "But I'm afraid my son has less tolerance for a memory I choose not to remember."

"I am so sorry." I held back the tears of humiliation.

"No, Sage. You are not to blame, nor should you apologize or feel it's your duty to take the blame for something your mother did so long ago."

She looked at Justin with purpose. "And this will never be mentioned again in or outside this room."

I didn't want to ask, for fear of dredging up more hurtful memories, but I had to know.

"Justin mentioned my family. What did the Andersons do to the McCaslands?"

"That too is in the past, and forgotten." Gavin shook his head.

I leaned forward, hoping to persuade him to tell me the story. "For Garrett and I to have the best chance for our marriage to work, we need to know all the gory details, regardless how horrible or hurtful. I don't want something later on down the road to pop up its ugly old head and cause us trouble."

Gavin glanced up at his wife. She gave a small nod.

He pursed his lips as if to say he didn't think it was a wise choice. "Like I said, hashing up the past won't do any one good. But since you insist."

"I do. I need to know if Garrett and I can know these things and still not let it affect our relationship." I glanced at Garrett.

"Nothing I hear will change my mind about you, Sage." He lifted the back of my hand, kissing it softly while watching me.

At the moment, I knew I loved Garrett beyond reason.

"All right, if you're set on it."

"I believe she is, Darling." Mrs. McCasland moved over to a chair and sat down.

"My grandfather and your great-grandfather were friends and partners in a farming co-op, along with several other farms. The McCaslands owned the combine and charged the co-op a percentage of the harvest for reaping the crop, which worked well for several years. When the drought hit, it took several farms under. Then came the rains and everyone in the area had a bumper crop."

Gavin grimaced, and shifted in his chair. "The night before Grandpa McCasland was to harvest the McCasland crops, the fields caught fire, along with two other farms nearby, losing the entire crop. By sheer fortune, our house and barns weren't touched. The next night, three other farms caught fire. Before the torching of the fields was over, eight farms in all had lost their crops."

He made a scoffing noise. "Miraculously, the Anderson's farm, which stood in the middle of all the other farms, was left unscathed.

"Rumor had it, old man Anderson set the fires, but there was no proof. My grandfather didn't believe the rumors. He harvested Anderson's crop. But when it came time to pay up, Anderson refused, even though he got better than top dollar for his crop.

"The three drought years and then losing the revenue from the co-op almost put the McCasland farm under. The co-op dissolved, and the McCaslands and Andersons parted ways."

I felt horrible over something totally out of my control.

Glancing over at Justin, Gavin drummed his fingers on the armrest. "Justin seems to have issues with old grievances. He takes the McCasland slights to heart and tries to right the wrongs in the world." Gavin smiled. "I believe that's why he's in law enforcement."

"I'm not a child, so please don't talk about me like I'm not here." Justin stood and then moved over to the window, looking out into the dusky evening.

"Point taken."

He turned to stare at me. "The Anderson history with the McCaslands hasn't been a good one. Particularly since it seems the Andersons always do their best to destroy the McCaslands. I don't want Garrett hurt."

"We were in grade school the last time you had to protect me." Garrett gave a wry chuckle while cupping my hand. "I don't need your protection."

He looked into my eyes, bathing me with his love.

"Especially where Sage is concerned. I love her, and she loves me."

I knew without a doubt he loved me regardless what went before.

I broke eye contact with Garrett. "Justin, I have no intention of hurting Garrett. But, if marrying Garrett will keep the two of you at odds, then I'll walk away."

"Sage—"

"There'll be no talk of walking away." Gavin shook his head. "Your part of our family now. And Justin?" He looked at his son expectantly.

"Dad's right. I was way out of line earlier today. I hope you can forgive me."

"I already have."

"Good." Kayla stood smiling. "I'm glad we have all the dirty laundry washed and out on the line. Who's ready for dessert."

"I've been ready since this afternoon when you pulled your Lemon Dream Cake from the oven and slapped my hand when I tried to filch a piece."

"Sage, dear, why don't you come with me. Let's leave these men to their own devices while we serve up the cake."

Garrett stood, pulling me to my feet. "Will you be all right?"

"Yes."

"And why wouldn't she be. I'm not going to gobble her up." His mother looked a little perturbed.

"Okay, then. I'll see you in a few minutes." He bent and gave me a quick kiss on the lips that sent my senses reeling and embarrassed me at the same time.

Out of the corner of my eye, I saw Justin give us an odd look. I hoped he still wasn't opposed to us because I knew I wanted to marry Garrett. However, if Justin was still opposed, I would walk away, regardless if giving up Garrett would leave me in a heap of a broken mess.

Chapter 25

Garrett

I wasn't sure about Justin. He didn't seem overly convincing to me. But as long as he didn't hassle Sage, I was fine.

Dad, Justin, and I conversed about the ranch and cattle. I was too distracted and worried Sage would feel out of place in the kitchen with Mom and Issy without me by her side. I almost laughed over that thought.

"What has you smiling?" Dad chuckled, rising from his chair. "As if I didn't already know. Let's go get our dessert and let Garrett get back to Sage's side."

"Sounds good to me." I was more than ready to see Sage again.

Dad walked out, but before Justin did, I caught him by the arm.

He wrinkled his brow.

"Are we good?"

Justin knew I referred to Sage.

"Yeah. We're good, as long as you're sure she isn't anything like her mother."

I laughed outright. "I can guarantee Sage is nothing like her mother. In fact, when you said the fruit doesn't fall far from the tree, you couldn't have been more off the mark. Sage has all of her grandmother's sweetness and none of Gabby's self-indulgence. Gabby's a piece of work. She didn't so much as lift a finger to help with her own mother's funeral arrangements. She left it all to Sage."

"You've got to be kidding." Justin's disgust was evident. "In that case, I'll see if I can't give the woman a ticket for some kind of violation while she's in town."

I laughed. "As much as I'd love for you to, please don't. I'm afraid Sage wouldn't be too happy with either of us if she found out about it."

Justin squinted at me. "You really love the girl, don't you?"

"That's an understatement. What I feel goes beyond love. I have the insatiable desire to never let her out of my sight. She's the other half of me that's been missing."

"All right. You've convinced me." He nodded at the doorway. "Let's get dessert before you start spouting poems to her virtues."

"Wait till you find the right one. You'll know exactly how I feel."

Justin laughed loudly. "No way, brother. You can be hogtied, but not me. I love my freedom too much to hand it over to someone who can squeeze the life out of me."

"Sage has added life, not squeezed it out of me. Just wait. You'll see when it happens to you."

When we entered the living room, Sage was conversing with Issy and Mom. Our dessert was sitting on the buffet. I was relieved that she didn't appear to be anxious and wanting to leave.

"Sage was just telling us how the two of you met." Issy sashayed over to one of the chairs in the living room, pulling her bare feet up and under her, then began eating her cake. "That's no way to treat a lady. So totally unlike you, bro."

I moved to where Sage stood.

She handed me a plate of cake, got one for herself and then followed the others into the living room.

"In my defense, I didn't do it on purpose. She didn't see me. I didn't see her ... until it was too late." I motioned for Sage to sit down and then slid down beside her on the couch, loving how she felt next to me.

"By then I was fighting mad." Sage laughed. "I was spitting and shoving lettuce every which way, trying to get up off the hard ground with my pride intact—which by then it wasn't."

The picture of Sage covered in lettuce had me smiling. "Yeah, I guess you're right. Bad form. But I'm totally satisfied with the results. I got the girl." I winked.

If the room hadn't been filled with curious eyes, I would have nuzzled her neck, and then planted one of the biggest kisses on her delectable lips. Instead, I shoveled a bite of cake into my mouth, totally unsatisfied.

"He paid dearly for my bushel of lettuce, though." She smiled up at me, her eyes sparkling.

"I'd say. That lettuce cost me an arm and leg, not to mention my male pride. For a moment there, it was iffy if she was going to sucker punch me or not."

Sage playfully socked my arm. "I'm not that kind of woman. Kick you maybe, but never bruise these delicate hands of mine."

The conversation turned to me when I was a little boy, everyone trying to outdo the other with embarrassing stories.

Seeing it was getting late, I said, "It's time to take Sage home so she can get some rest."

Everyone stood, saying their goodbyes. When Justin stepped up, my first reaction was to step in front of Sage. Her slight tug on my hand, made me stop. I figured, if he insulted Sage, I'd plant him a facer, regardless if we were in my folks' house.

"I apologize for earlier today. I was way out of line and I knew better. I hope you will forgive me, and we can be friends."

Sage tilted her head to the side looking up at Justin studying him curiously. "I forgive you. But you've got to promise me one thing."

I watched the exchange and saw the sparkle in her eyes. I wondered what she was up to.

"What's that." Justin's brow was tight.

"That you won't stop me every time you see me and give me a ticket for some small infraction." She raised her brow giving him a mischievous look. "In fact, isn't there some kind of family exemption you can give me?"

Justin's face turned a deep red. "My threat was louder than my bite. I would have never followed through. I was just trying to scare you off." He held out his hand. "But I'm sure glad you don't scare easily. Truce?"

"Truce." Sage shook Justin's hand. "Are all of you McCaslands boys as tenacious as these two?" She motioned to me and Justin.

"They're worse," Issy piped up. "Any guy I date, they all gang up on him. By the time they're through with him, he never comes back. Maybe now, I'll get a reprieve."

"Not likely." We all agreed, while giving Issy the evil eye.

"Issy." Sage wrapped her arm through mine.

It was the first non-conscious act of belonging to me Sage had ever shown.

"Don't worry about Garrett. I'll keep him busy." She smiled up at me. "But these other three, I'm afraid I'll be of no help, unless I can use a guilt-trip on Justin."

All the brothers started teasing Issy, while Sage continued to stand up for her, telling us we were horrible to treat our sister like this. In that moment, I knew Sage belonged to the family.

By the time I got her in the truck, it was already going on ten.

When we arrived at her house, I helped Sage down, pulling her into my arms, up close and personal.

"I don't know about you, but I've been hungry all night long."

She looked at me puzzled like. "After that meal and the cake, you can't be hungry. Where do you put it all?"

"I'm not hungry for food, but for this."

Before she could say anything, I dipped my head and captured her lips. At first the kiss was soft and gentle, her lip pliable beneath mine. The taste of her drove me wild. Before I knew it, my hunger for Sage was insatiable.

Tilting my head, I deepened our kiss, wanting her to know just how much I loved her and needed her in my life forever.

I pulled back more shaken than I believed imaginable. Resting my forehead on hers, feeling our hearts beat out the age-old rhythm of love, our breathing slowed. I looked down into Sage's face, lit only by the full moon overhead and the backdrop of the porch light. Her face was flush, her lips swollen.

"If anyone would have told me I could love someone as much as I love you, I would have scoffed at them. I've fallen under your spell. Your beauty takes my breath away. And I count the seconds I'm away from you." I squeezed her up close to me then released her. "I love you, Sage Anderson. And will until the day I die.

"Garrett, I—"

Afraid she was going to tell me something I didn't want to hear, I placed my finger over her lips.

"No, leave it for another time." I blew out my breath, hoping to relieve the pressure of the love building up inside me. My chest ached with wanting.

"I won't come in, because if I do, I don't believe I could leave."

Interlocking our hands, I walked her to her door. "Unless you have other plans, I'd like to drive you to the church tomorrow."

"I would love that. And will you sit with me?"

"If you want me to."

"I do. I need your strength. I believe Grams would be happy if she knew you were beside me."

We stopped at the porch. I turned to face her, touching her chin, lifting it enough for her to look into my eyes.

"I will be beside you every minute unless you tell me otherwise."

Again, I dipped my head, capturing her warm lips. This time the kiss was soft and gentle, stirring the flame in my heart.

I let her go, then moved back against the newel post. "I love you. And that will never change." Nodding, I said, "Go on inside before I change my mind."

She gave me a sassy smile. "How soon do you think would be a reasonable and respectful period of time for us to get married?"

Unable to believe my ears, I shook my head. "You do know what you're asking."

"I do, and I love you."

"The day after tomorrow." I smiled wickedly, moving away from the post, gathering her in my arms again.

She giggled, tucking her head. "How about next month? Do you think people would think it strange, with my grandmother's passing and all?"

"What do we care? As long as we are together, married, and living in our own home. What others say has no bearing on what we do."

"You've got a point." She played with one of the buttons on my shirt. "But what do you think? Is it too soon?"

I gave her a squeeze, wanting to run off with her tonight, but knew the idea was unreasonable.

"In my opinion, today isn't soon enough. But I'll compromise." I kissed her on the tip of her nose before continuing. "Next month will work out fine if that's what you want."

"I do."

"Then next month it is." My mind began planning. "As you pack boxes, the stuff you want to keep can be moved into my house. We'll have the farm house cleared out and ready by the date your stepfather set, and our wedding as soon as you like. So no, next month is not too soon."

"I don't want our wedding to be big or formal, though my mother will try to insist."

I pulled her over to the bench on the porch and had her sit down beside me.

"This isn't your mother's wedding. This is ours. Whatever you want or don't want, I'll make it happen. No one is going to make you do what you don't want to do as long as I'm around."

"Thanks, Garrett." She bit her lower lip. "If you don't mind, I'd rather not say anything to Gabby, at least not yet. I'd rather tell her next week after we have our wedding date set."

"Whatever you want." I put my arm around her and felt her relax against me.

We sat quietly listening to the crickets, as a soft breeze filled the night air. Her breathing was slow and even. I felt the slight tremble before I realized she was crying.

"Ah, Baby." I pulled her up tight against my chest. "What's wrong. It's not about marrying me, is it?"

"No, and yes." She sniffled. "I love you and want to marry you. But I so wanted Grams to be at my wedding, and now she won't be." She sniffed soundly, wiping her eyes. "Garrett, I miss her so much."

I held her not knowing what to say or do.

"You know what she always told me?" She sniffled.

"No, what?"

"She always said God would send me a man who would love me. He did. But she's not here to know her prayers were answered."

"Ah, Baby, she knows. I think she knew the first day I came knocking on your backdoor. That's why I believe she wasn't troubled about you any longer. She knew I would love and care for you."

Sage looked up at me. "Do you really think so?"

"I wouldn't say it if I didn't believe it."

She touched my cheek. "Thank you, Garrett. Not just for the words but for loving me."

"That's something I couldn't stop."

She reached up and pulled my head toward hers. This kiss was different from all the others. It was a mixture of sadness, joy, and happiness, and so sweet.

When our kiss ended, I knew beyond a shadow of a doubt, God had sent this slip of a woman to me. She could be touched by sorrow yet show love.

She could be tenacious when she had to be and still show her soft side. But what I loved most, Sage had the capacity to love me with her whole heart, holding back nothing.

"Garrett?" She nestled her head on my chest again.

"Yes, love."

Her body became taut. I felt the tension growing in her body.

"I sure hope you're strong because Gabby is going to do her best to tear us apart."

"That's something no one will ever do, not even Ms. Strong-Willed Gabby."

Chapter 26

Sage

The funeral, even the graveside service was simple, sweet, and beautiful, just like Grams' wanted. There were only two close calls.

The first happened when Garrett walked me down the aisle and sat next to me. Gabby's back stiffened, her nose rose higher as she practically glared at him. Thankfully she didn't ask him to move because I would have moved with him.

The second close call was when Gabby told Garrett I'd ride with them to the cemetery. He looked at me and must have read my thoughts, because he told her I was riding with him, and then led me to his car.

The drive back to the church for the luncheon prepared by all of Gram's friends, was quiet. Garrett was giving me my space—to either talk or not, my choice.

"Garrett, I'm sorry about Gabby. But I did warn you."

"Listen, Babe, I can handle Gabby. However, I'll follow your lead. If you want me to stay, I'll stay. If you want me to go, I'll go. Gabby has no say in the matter."

I grinned, knowing Gabby would have a lot to say, but I wouldn't spoil the fun for Garrett.

"Thanks. Don't leave my side." I motioned to the left. "The fellowship hall is in the back."

Garrett pulled up beside another car, turned off the engine, and then looked at me. "You okay?"

"I'm fine."

"Then let's go in. But first, I've got to do this." He pulled me toward him and kissed me.

The kiss was over before I wanted it to be. Garrett hopped out of the truck, then came around to help me down.

When we entered the rec hall, several of Grams friends came up to me to give their condolences while casting admiring glances at Garrett. I introduced him to the women as my fiancé. Gladys, at age 78, the youngest of the group, winked at me.

She picked up my hand and looked at the diamond ring Garrett had given me.

"Ladies, it appears our little Sage has captured herself one fine specimen of a man. There's to be a wedding to which we will be invited." Her questioning look had me smiling.

"Of course you will be. Grams would want you there, and so do we."

The other three women started talking and congratulating.

"I believe, Sage dear, you're Grams would have been happy about your beau. In fact, she's probably dancing in heaven right this minute."

"I hope so."

Gladys patted my hand. "You can believe it. I don't know how many times Adeline said to me, 'Gladys, I'll be so happy when the right young man comes around asking to marry my Sage. She needs a good man who will love her and watch over her.' And it looks like you've got exactly that."

"Thank you, Gladys. Your kind words mean a lot to me."

"It's nothing but the truth." She patted my cheek.

"Thank you, ladies. You're very kind."

For a minute, I thought Garrett's gorgeous smile would give the ladies heart palpitations.

When the women moved away, he leaned down by my ear. "Seems Grams' friends are in favor of me."

I laughed. "They were very much in favor of my guy. They couldn't keep their eyes off you. For a moment there, I wasn't sure if they were here to see me, or you."

He chuckled. "That Gladys was kind of cute. I wonder if she's ever thought about becoming a cougar?"

I elbowed him in the side. "Not hardly."

"There you are." Gabby walked up, looking less than pleasant, while Robert stood off to the side.

"Robert and I will be leaving in a few minutes. I need to know when you will be moving into the apartment."

"I won't be moving into Dallas. And thanks, Robert, but I won't be taking the job either."

Gabby's glare landed on Garrett. "I assume this is your doing?"

"I'm afraid it—"

Squeezing Garrett's arm, I let him know I would handle Gabby this time.

"It was my decision. And I don't believe this is either the time or place for this discussion."

I turned to leave, then stopped. "I'll give you a call later this evening."

"I demand to know why you've made an about-face since yesterday."

"This conversation isn't going to happen here or now." I started to walk off.

"Gabby, we wish to offer our condolences."

Kayla walked up with Gavin. I stopped, not knowing what would happen next.

My mother clamped her mouth shut, then gave a wooden smile.

"Thank you for coming. Mother's passing was such an upset, as I'm sure Sage has mentioned."

"Yes." Kayla gave me a sweet smile.

"And what do you think about Sage and Garrett?" Gabby cocked her one brow.

"We are all excited. Sage is such a sweet girl. She fits in well with our family."

"The Andersons and the McCaslands get together at last." Gabby's tone sounded condescending and a little bitter.

I stared at her, trying to figure out why Gabby would even bring up the past.

Gavin looked ready to tear into Gabby.

"Let me introduce you to my husband." Gabby turned, motioning at Robert. "This is Robert Stanford. He's the president of National Bank and Trust, Dallas. Robert, this is Gavin and Kayla Anderson. The three of us went to high school together and have quite a history."

Again Gavin stiffened, but then I noticed a gentle squeeze of Kayla's hand on Gavin's arm.

While they went through the formalities, I watched Gabby and wondered what she was up to. She was being unusually catty. And there was a hint of something else behind her demeanor that I couldn't quite put my finger on.

"Robert offered Sage a good job, but for some reason she has it in her head not to take the position." She gave a brief glance in Garrett's direction and laughed, which sounded false and grating. "I think she believes she can live on love."

Aw, at last. She was going for the jugular.

"You can rest easy, *Gabby*—"

Garrett's interjection startled me and everyone else. And then to call her Gabby—*wow!* He was giving it back as good as she gave.

"I earn more than enough to allow Sage to live on love and my income at the same time." Garrett narrowed his gaze in Gabby's direction. "As my wife, she won't have to work if she doesn't want to. I am more than capable of supporting her in whatever manner she wishes."

"*Humph.* That's good to know because she certainly doesn't have any money of her own." Gabby smiled at the McCaslands.

Gabby released a sigh, her nose in the air. "Robert has a very important meeting this afternoon and we need to leave." She smiled at the McCaslands. "We must get together again soon, especially since we will shortly be quasi-related, if it happens at all."

She grabbed hold of Robert's arm. "Sage, I'll expect a call from you later tonight."

I didn't answer, just watched her walk off, sashaying her tush with her back ramrod straight.

"Good riddance. I'm glad that's over." I remembered who was standing there with me. I bit my lip, then smiled at my soon-to-be in-laws. "I'm sorry. At times, she can be a handful. And believe it or not, she was on her best behavior just now."

"I hope you'll warn me when she isn't, so I can watch my back." Garrett laughed.

"Oh, you'll know." I chuckled.

Addressing his parents, I said, "I apologize. Gabby and I don't exactly see eye-to-eye on things. I'm sure she thinks I'm being difficult."

"You don't have to explain your mother to us. If you remember, we have a history with her."

"I do remember. That's why I'm trying to smooth things over. I don't want you to be offended and think that I'm remotely like her."

"We're not. And dear, you could never be like your mother. She's one of a kind." Kayla smiled as she grabbed her husband's arm. "Now, shall we go and get some of that great smelling food the ladies have prepared?"

Garrett motioned to his folks. "Go on ahead. We'll be right with you."

"We'll save you a place." Kayla patted my arm.

When they were out of earshot, Garrett turned me to face him. "When lunch is over, I'd like for us to go somewhere, maybe out to the pond on my ranch, and have a talk. Do you have the time?"

"You're not mad are you?" I bit my lower lip.

"No, I'm not mad." He ran his fingers over the wrinkle in my brow. "However, there are a few things we need to discuss before you talk with your mother tonight."

"All right." I looked around. Several people were watching us. "When we're done here, will you run me home so I can change?"

"Better yet, I'll drop you off, run home to change, then come back to pick you up."

"That works. Now, shall we go get some food? I think I finally have an appetite."

By the time we had gone down the lineup of food and loaded our plates, Garrett's *some things to discuss* was blown out of proportion in my mind. My stomach was in a state of rebellion.

Love by the Bushel   Janice Olson

Lord, whatever it is, please don't let be that he is having second thoughts. It would break my heart

Chapter 27

Garrett

I took the dirt road that led a short distance from my house. Sage hadn't said much from the time I'd picked her up.

Uncertain if her quiet mood was due to Grams' funeral or she was stewing over something else, I remained quiet, figuring she would tell me in due time.

We topped the knoll. I stopped, allowing Sage to get the full effect of the scene. Her intake of breath said it all.

Stretched out in front of us was my pride and joy, my place to go when I needed to think and work out a problem.

The ten-acre pond, surrounded by huge oak trees, sparkled and glistened like a diamond in the sun. The ancient, gnarled branches of the oaks reached for the sky and stretched out over thick green grass, providing shade from the summer heat.

To one side of the lake sat a nice-sized gazebo I had built a couple of years back. There was also a barbecue pit large enough to roast a whole side of beef or a pig, and picnic tables and benches scattered about.

"I never dreamt a place like this existed on your farm." She glanced at me smiling, her eyes full of wonder. Then she turned back to look out the window again. "Oh, Garrett, it's gorgeous."

"Glad you like it."

"Like it? I love it. This would be a wonderful place to get away and think or just relax."

I grinned and took my foot off the brake, coasting the rest of the way down the small hill before stopping under one of the trees.

Sage swung the door open and jumped down. She ran to the gazebo and then slowly mounted the steps, looking around.

Grabbing the quilt from the backseat of the truck, I followed her. When I entered the gazebo, she turned around. Her face aglow, she ran into my arms, hugging me.

"This is the best surprise."

Immediately, I saw her mortification. She dropped her arms and stepped back, turning her back to me, glancing out at the lake.

"Sage, what's wrong?"

"Nothing. You said you wanted to talk. Are we talking here?" She motioned about the gazebo without looking at me.

"This is as good a place as any. Or we can make use of the quilt you brought and go down by the lake. Which would you prefer?"

She noticed the quilt over my arm. "The lake would be nice."

"The lake it is then."

We positioned the quilt on the ground and then sat down.

"If you're having second thoughts about marrying me, I understand completely."

I blinked a couple of times, scowling at her. "Where did that come from?"

"When Gabby offended you and then left, you said we needed to talk before I called her. So I just thought ..."

"Come here, you." I dragged Sage over next to me and gathered her in my arms, and then kissed her until I needed to break it off. It was either stop kissing her or let things get completely out of hand. I broke the kiss.

Her face was flushed but not from the heat. Her breathing was as heavy as mine. I knew she wanted me as much as I wanted her. But I also knew we would wait until she wore my wedding band and my name, even if I didn't like waiting.

"I guess that means we're still getting married."

"You guessed right. And Sage ..." I waited until she looked at me.

"I don't want to hear you spout any such nonsense ever again. Do we have an agreement?"

She nodded.

I gently brushed the stray hair from her face, loving the feel of her soft skin beneath my fingertips. I rested my hand on her cheek.

"You know something?"

"No, what?"

"You've got to be the most beautiful creature God ever created. Your hair, your face, your eyes, even your body is perfection. I can't believe you waited for me to come along."

"Silly, I didn't know you existed until you plowed into me at the market." She grinned. "But I'm so glad you did." She leaned over and kissed me on the cheek.

Wanting to kiss her thoroughly, I opted to hold her hand.

"You're like a powerful magnet. I can't resist you."

Her smile was so sweet, yet I saw that devilish twinkle in her eyes. She knew exactly how she affected me. "You wanted to talk? About what?"

I cleared my throat, tamping down my desire, while at the same time hoping I wouldn't make Sage upset.

"Where Gabby is concerned, I don't want her to come between us."

"She won't. I won't let her."

"Good. But she brought up some issues I want to address, which, to my way of thinking is none of her business, except for her to know I can care for you properly."

I motioned around at my farm. "I own all of this land free and clear, and I make a good living, not just off the land, but with my teaching and speaking abilities." I cleared my throat feeling self-conscious not wanting to brag. "I'm not trying to boast, but I want you to know, you and our children will never want for anything."

"When are you going to get down to the part where you will lavish me in furs, diamonds, and cars so I can tell you, I don't want any of those things. If you were a pauper without a dime to your name, I'd marry you anyway."

"I appreciate that. But I'm nowhere close to being a pauper. With my income, I can support you and as many kids as you want to give me."

"That's good to know. Because, being an only child, I would like a dozen children."

Looking doubtful, I teased, "You may want to rethink that. I have four siblings, and believe me, it's not all it's cracked up to be. Look at Justin." I wiggled my brows, smiling. "But, if that's what you want, I'll be glad to oblige."

I gathered her up in my arms and rolled with her, then stopped, looking down into her face.

"One thing for sure, I'm thinking this month is going to be a real test of my strength."

Worried, she stared at me. "Why? Because of Gabby?"

"Nah, she's a piece of cake." I tweaked her nose. "But keeping my hands off you, now that will be the real challenge."

Chapter 28

Sage

I woke with a start at the unfamiliar surroundings, then stretched, smiling.

I was in Garrett's bed, or at least his bed while growing up in his parents' house.

Today was our wedding day.

The thought brought joy as I bounded out of bed to open the drapes. I stood looking out at the McCasland's backyard, thankful for a beautiful sunny day. Below me, the ornamental pond glistened in the early morning light.

It didn't take long to pull my hair up in a ponytail and get dressed in my warmups, and then make my way quietly down to the kitchen. The smell of fresh brewed coffee filled my nose.

After pouring myself a cup, I slipped out the back door to the garden, needing some time to myself before the business of the day began.

I found a beautiful little white arbor bench next to a tree and small waterfall. I sat down to enjoy a few moments alone while wondering if Garrett was awake yet.

"Hey," My soon-to-be sister-in-law, Issy, appeared, cup in hand. "I thought I saw you from the window."

"It's me." I smiled, glad that Issy and I had hit it off so well. I finally had the sister I'd always wanted. "I thought I'd drink up the peace and quiet before all the craziness begins."

"I hear ya."

"Have a seat." I scooted over, giving plenty of room for Issy to sit down.

"I just hope I find someone that is as meant for me as you are for Garrett." She giggled. "None of my silly friends would have ever made him as happy as he is with you."

Pleased at her conclusion, I hugged her. "Thanks. And thanks for being such a sweet sister-in-law. I couldn't have packed up Gram's house and pulled the wedding off if it hadn't been for all your help."

"Hey, I enjoyed all the planning and decorating. That kind of stuff is right down my alley." She took a sip of her coffee.

"You're good at it. So good, in fact, you should seriously think about becoming a wedding coordinator or events planner. You're a natural."

"I've given some thought about doing something like that, but I'm not sure what my folks and my brothers would think. And …" Issy wrinkled her nose. "I'm not sure I could make a living at it. At Matt's law firm, I'm earning good money, and at the same time utilizing my business degree managing his office."

"But are you happy?"

She shrugged, teetering her hand back and forth. "For now, yeah. But for long term, no."

"Once we're back from our honeymoon, I'm going to need something to do to keep busy. Garrett wants me to take some time off before looking for a job. Who knows, maybe we can form a partnership."

"Sounds good to me." Issy looked at her watch. "I've gotta run. I promised I'd meet Christa to help set up the food tables. If our cousin wasn't a choral director at the Primrose High, she'd be another one good for that type business. Her catering skills are to die for."

She gave me a hug. "I'll be back in time to help you dress. See ya."

Issy was off like a little flittering butterfly.

***

Garrett

The quintet's music filled the air as I followed the minister down the aisle of green, past the intimate gathering of family and friends. I stopped, but the minister proceeded up the steps, then turned, standing at the center of the gazebo facing the crowd. My three brothers, arranged by age, tux and all, fell in line next to me while I waited for Sage to walk down the aisle.

While I watched for Mom's Suburban to top the hill, I waited for the teasing to begin.

"There's still time to back out." Matt joked under his breath.

"A ring in the nose comes next." Justin laughed.

Matt shook his head. "No, it's the ol' ball and chain that comes after the ceremony."

"Hey, bro." Nick leaned out from the others to look at me. "Maybe she's a runaway bride. Should I go check?"

"Ha. Ha. I didn't know my best men were a bunch of comedians." My heart accelerated. "Here's the car now."

Dad parked the car and then ran around to open the back door for Sage.

Her bridesmaids hovered around her, helping her out of the car. They concealed my vision of her. All I saw was some soft white flimsy cloth take flight in the wind, and then one of the girls caught it, bringing it down and around Sage.

Gabby and Robert wouldn't be attending Gabby's only child's wedding. Her excuse, a last minute business trip that couldn't be cancelled.

I wanted to drag Gabby here and hogtie her to a chair, but Sage wouldn't let me. My folks stepped up and showered her with love as if she were one of their own. Still I knew Sage was crushed.

The music changed—the cue that the bridesmaids were to line up and start walking down the aisle. Thinking I'd get my first glimpse of Sage, I didn't. My father shielded her this time.

When the wedding march began, Dad backed up and held out his arm.

Sage was exquisite. The most beautiful woman I could ever imagine. Slipping her arm through Dad's, they began walking toward me. She smiled, her face glowing like the morning sun.

Her white dressed accentuated her figure, flaring out below her hips. Her veil rambled out behind her with the light breeze. In her hand, she carried a small bouquet of red roses with honeysuckle trailing down in front of her dress—she explained both flowers represented our love.

She wasn't walking fast enough as far as I was concerned. At this rate, I wouldn't have her to myself before nightfall—totally unacceptable.

I chuckled when I saw Grams' friends all waving at Sage while dabbing their eyes.

If God allowed loved ones to look down from heaven on special days like this, I knew Grams would be up there smiling.

"Finally," I breathed out as I walked forward to meet Sage.

She chuckled, rolling her eyes. "I'm here now."

Under my breath, I said, "Laugh, if you will. It has been an extremely long day while I waited for this moment to arrive." I grinned. "I love you."

Sage bit her lower lip on the verge of happy tears.

Thankfully, I now knew the difference between her happy tears and sad ones.

I walked with her up the steps and inside the gazebo, where we stood before the minister—Sage's idea.

As we exchanged our vows, I couldn't thank God enough for literally throwing Sage into my path that fateful day. I shuddered to think what my life would have been without her.

My gaze never left her face as we repeated our vows—*to honor, love and be faithful and true as long as we both live.*

When the minister finally said you may kiss the bride, I dipped Sage backwards over my arm and gave her a kiss that hopefully tingled her toes.

The clapping and wolf whistles brought me to my senses. But I couldn't help but wish I could get Sage out of here and begin our honeymoon, right this minute.

Tomorrow, we would fly out of Dallas to the Virgin Islands for two wonderful weeks of marital bliss, after our night's stay at the Omni Hotel. Just the thought of having Sage all to myself, without any restraints, was driving me crazy.

I hugged her up close and leaned down next to her ear. "Can we leave now, Mrs. McCasland?"

"No, but soon. Real soon, Mr. McCasland." She winked at me.

"That's my gal."

"Oh, and Garrett?"

"Yeah?"

"Thank you for loving me. I am the happiest woman alive."

She reached up and planted a kiss on me that caused my brothers to start a stream of wolf whistles that I felt sure could be heard all the way to Primrose.

We pulled back, smiling. I grabbed her hand and then turned to the audience.

"Thank you for coming and being a part of our special day. The tables are loaded with food. So eat up. And while you're eating the band will entertain you as my bride and I make the rounds to thank you personally for sharing our special day."

People began mingling and heading to the buffet.

Unable to keep my hands off my wife, I grabbed her up, twirled her around, breathing in her scent.

"Wife, you're driving me wild. When can we leave Primrose for our honeymoon."

"Soon." Her eyes sparkled.

"But that's not soon enough."

Her laughter warmed my heart. There was no doubt in my mind that God had placed Sage in my path that day at the farmers' market. And I knew Sage and I would live a lifetime of love filled with wonderful memories and no regrets.

You turned my mourning into dancing;

You took my sackcloth and
clothed me with garments of joy. Psalm 31:11 ISV

Dear Reader,

I hope you enjoyed book one in the series: *The McCaslands of Primrose, Texas—Garrett's journey to happiness.*

Isn't it odd how love comes along when a person least expects it. Kind of like Garrett and Sage's first meeting. Who would have thought they would ever get along, let alone fall in love and get married after their first meeting?

Book two in the McCasland Series, *"Arrested by Love,"* picks up with brother number three, Officer Justin McCasland, one of Primrose's finest, except when it came to Sage. He nearly sabotaged Sage and Garrett's happily-ever-after. Though Justin came off looking tough and mean, he redeemed himself in the end. I believe you'll fall in love with him in *"Arrested by Love."* He's a soft ol' teddy bear with a big heart on its way to being challenged—at least his vow to stay single is certainly going to be tested.

Sage convinces her friend from college, Livy (Olivia Martin) to move to Primrose. Livy takes the plunge ... lock, stock, and ... eight young girls in tow between the ages of fifteen and seventeen. What's that all about, you ask? Now, that's the real question, and it's a secret for now. All I can say on the subject, it makes life interesting for Justin and Livy. And you can betcha, someone is going to be arrested and locked up in the calaboose.

Thanks, again for reading *"Love by the Bushel."* Start looking for Justin's story 2017.

Until next time, read a good book and become enriched.

Blessings,

Janice Olson
www.JaniceOlson.com

To keep in the know about my new releases and giveaways, email me at:

Janice at Janice Olson dot com and in the subject line type *"Janice's Readers Club"* and I'll add you to my list.

Love by the Bushel   *Janice Olson*

www.ingramcontent.com/pod-product-compliance
Lightning Source LLC
Chambersburg PA
CBHW061544170626
46811CB00001B/77